KEN BRUEN

hails from the west of Irel
his time between south London and
Galway. His past includes drunken brawls
in Vietnam, a stretch of four months in a
south American gaol, a PhD in
metaphysics and three of the most
acclaimed crime novels of our times.

A White Arrest is the first book in the
landmark WHITE TRILOGY.

A White Arrest

Ken Bruen

BLOODLINES

First Published in Great Britain in 1998,
Revised edition 2005 by:
The Do-Not Press Ltd
16 The Woodlands
London SE13 6TY
www.thedonotpress.com

A paperback original.

ISBN 1 899344 41 1

British Library Cataloguing in Publication Data. A catalogue
record for this book is available from the British Library.

h g f e d c b

Printed and bound in Great Britain by Bookmarque Ltd

FOR MICHAEL BURT

a white arrest

the pinnacle of a policeman's career
— Sir Robert Peel

the big one cancels all the previous shit
— Detective Sergeant Brant

R&B they were called. If Chief Inspector Roberts was like the Rhythm, then Brant was the darkest Blues. *Pig ignorant, more like*, was also said.

On Robert's desk was a phone, a family photo, a bronze and wood scroll, which read:

> On Easter Monday 1901, the Rev. James Charmers stepped ashore on Goaribari Island, off the Southern Coast of New Guinea, intent on converting the islanders. The Goas ran down to meet him, clubbed him senseless, then they cut him into small pieces, boiled him and ate him that afternoon.

It was all you needed to know for police work, he said.

WPC Falls contemplated the sugared doughnut. It sat like a fat reprimand next to her coffee. Another WPC joined her, said: 'Now,. that's temptation.'

'Hiya, Rosie.'

'Hiya – so, are you going to eat it?'

She didn't know, said: 'I dunno.'

Falls was the wet dream of the nick. Leastways, she hoped she was. A little over 5' 6", she was the loaded side of plump, but it suited her. Seeing her, the adjectives of ravishment sprang to mind: lush, ripe, buxom, available. The last in hopeful neon.

She gave a low laugh, lewd and knowing.

Rosie said: 'What?'

'You know Andrews?'

'From Brixton nick?'

'Yeah, him. I gave him the old con last night – you know the shit men believe.'

Rosie laughed, asked:

'Not the "Sex has to be spiritual for a woman, she can't just fuck and fly"?'

Falls was laughing out loud, into it now, the story carrying her.

'Yeah, I explained how we have to be emotionally involved. The dim sod went for it completely.'

She took another wedge of the doughnut, let her eyes dance with sugared delight and went for the kill:

'Worse – he believed me when I said size doesn't matter.'

Rosie was trying not to laugh too loud. In a canteen full of men, women's laughter was a downright threat. She held up her thumb and index finger, measuring off a quarter inch, asked: 'Look familiar?'

Falls shrieked.

'You had him too, wanton cow.'

'Well, he was quick, I'll say that for him.'

Falls shoved the remains of the doughnut to her, said: 'Seeing as we've shared the little things…'

WPC Falls had curly hair, cut short in almost dyke style. It emphasised her dark eyes. A snub nose gave her an appearance of eagerness and a thin mouth saved her from outright prettiness. Her legs were her worst feature and a constant bane. Suddenly serious, she said:

'I was thirty-two years of age before I realised that when my dad said, "I'll kill myself and the girl with me", that it wasn't love – just drink talk.'

'Is he still alive, your dad?'

'Some days, but never on weekends.'

'Sounds like my Jack. Ever since he got laid off he's been legless.'

'The stronger sex, eh?'

'So they think.'

Rosie had what are termed 'grateful looks'. She was grateful if anybody looked. Few did, not even Jack.

*

Leroy Baker was a poor example of strength. As he did the fifth line of coke he roared: 'Ar…gh…rr. Fuck!'

Then stomped his unlaced LA sneaker, adding: 'That shit's good.'

He surveyed his flat. Awash in everything that money could buy. Leroy had a mountain of cash. The drug business was flourishing and he felt a little tasting of the product couldn't hurt, good for business in fact. That he was now hopelessly addicted got away from him.

He'd say: 'Keeps me sharp – a man in de biz gotta stay focused.'

A pounding on his door failed to register at first. The cocaine pounding of his heart had deafened him. As the hinges gave way and the door moved, he started to pay attention. Then the door came in and four men charged into his domain. He had a vague impression of boiler suits and balaclavas but fixed on the bats – baseball bats.

It was the last focus he had.

Twenty minutes later he was dangling from a lamppost, his neck broken. A white placard round his neck proclaimed:

E IS ENOUGH

Leroy was the first.

Down the street, a lone LA sneaker gave witness to the direction from which he'd been dragged. As the 'E' story built, it would be alleged one of the gang whistled as he worked. The tune suggested was 'Leaning on a Lamppost at the Corner of the Street'.

Like so much to come it was shrouded in wish fulfilment and revulsion – the two essentials for maximum publicity.

'a blue collar soul'

Roberts picked up the phone, answered:
'Chief Inspector.'
He never tired of the title.

'John? John, is that you?'

'Yes, dear.'

'I must say you sound terribly formal, quite the man of importance.'

He tried to hold his temper, stared at the receiver, took a deep breath and asked: 'Was there something?'

'The dry-cleaning, can you pick it up?'

'Pick it up yourself!'

And he put the phone down, lifted it up again and punched a digit.

'Yes, sir?'

'I've just had a call from my wife.'

'Oh sorry sir, she said it was urgent.'

'Never put her through. Was I vague in my last request?'

'Vague, sir?'

'Did I lack some air of command? Did I perhaps leave a loophole of doubt that said, "Sometimes it's OK to put the bitch through"?'

'No, sir – sorry sir. Won't happen again.'

'Let's not make too much of it. If it happens again, you'll be bundling homeys on Railton Road for years to come. Now piss off.'

He moved from behind his desk and contemplated his reflection in a half mirror. A photo of former England cricket captain Mike Atherton in one corner with the caption:

Roberts was sixty-two and at full stance he looked impos-
ing. Recently he found it more difficult to maintain. A sag
whispered at his shoulders. It whispered 'old'.

His body was muscular but it took work. More than he
wanted to give. A full head of hair was steel grey and he felt
the lure of the Grecian alternative – but not yet. Brown eyes
that were never gentle and a Roman nose. Daily he said, 'I
hate that fuckin' nose.' A headbutt from a drunk had pushed
it off-centre to give the effect of a botched nose job.
According to his wife, his mouth was unremarkable till he
spoke, then it was ugly. He got perverse joy from that.

Now he hit the intercom, barked: 'Get me Falls.'

'Ahm…'

'Are you deaf?'

'Sorry, sir. I'm not sure where she's at.'

'Where she's at! What is this? A bloody commune? You're
a policeman, go and find her. go and find her now and don't
ever let me hear that hippy shit again.'

'Yes, sir.'

Five minutes later a knock and Falls entered, straighten-
ing her tunic, crumbs floating to the floor. They both watched
the descent. He said:

'Picking from a rich man's platter perhaps?'

She smiled. 'Hardly, sir.'

'I have a job for you.'

'Yes, sir?'

He rummaged through his desk, produced a few pink
tickets, flipped them towards her.

She said, 'Dry-cleaning tickets?'

'Well identified; collect them on your lunch hour, eh?'

She let them lie, said: 'Hardly, sir – I mean, it's not in my
brief to be valet or something.'

He gave her a look of pure indignation.

'Jeez, you don't think I'll collect then, do you? How
would that look? Man of my rank poncing about a dry-clean-
ers?'

'With all due respect, sir, I—'

He cut her off.

'If you want to stay on my good side, love, don't bugger me about.'

She considered standing on her dignity, making a gesture for the sisterhood, telling him, with respect, to shove it, then thought, yeah sure.

And picked up the tickets, said: 'I'll need paying.'

'Don't we all, love – where's Brant?'

Later: Roberts had just parked his car and was starting to walk when a man stepped out of the shadows. A big man. He bruised out of his track suit and all of it muscle.

He said: 'I'm going to need your money, mate, and probably your watch if it's not a piece of shit.'

Roberts, feeling so tired, said: 'Would it help your decision to know I'm a copper?'

'A bit, but not enough. I've been asking people for money all day, asking nice and they treated me like dirt. So, now it's no more Mr Nice Guy. Hand it over, pal.'

'Okay, as you can see, I'm no spring chicken, and fit? I'm fit for nowt, but I've a real mean streak. No doubt you'll hurt me a lot but I promise you, I'll hurt you fucking back.'

The man considered, stepped forward, then spat: 'Ah bollocks, forget it. All right.'

'Forget. No. I don't think so. Get off my manor, pal, you're too big to miss.'

After Roberts moved away, the man considered putting a brick through his windshield, or slash the tyres or some fuck. But that bastard would come after him. Oh yes, a relentless cold fuck. Best leave well enough alone.

He said: 'You were lucky, mate.'

Who exactly he meant was unclear.

When Roberts got back home, he had to lean against the door. His legs turned to water and tiny tremors hit him. A voice asked: 'Not having a turn are you, Dad?'

Sarah, his fifteen-year-old daughter, supposedly at boarding school, a very expensive one, in the coronary area. It didn't so much drain his resources as blast a hole through them – wide and unstoppable. He tried for composure.

'Whatcha doing home, not half term already?'

'No. I got suspended.'

'What? What on earth for? Got to get me a drink.'

He poured a sensible measure of Glenlivet, then added to it, took a heavy slug and glanced at his daughter. She was in that eternal moment of preciousness between girl and woman. She loved and loathed her dad in equal measure. He looked closer, said:

'Good grief, are those hooks in your lips?'

'It's fashion, Dad.'

'Bloody painful, I'd say. Is that why you're home?'

'Course not. Mum says not to tell you, I didn't do nuff-ink.'

Roberts sighed: an ever-constant cloud of financial ruin hung over his head, just to teach her how to pronounce 'nothing'. And she said it as if she'd submerged south of the river and never surfaced.

He picked up the phone while Sarah signalled 'later' and headed upstairs.

'This is DI Roberts. Yeah, I'm home and a guy tried to mug me on my own doorstep. What? What is this? Did I apprehend him? Get me DS Brant and get a car over here to pick up this guy. He's a huge white fella in a dirty green tracksuit. Let Brant deal with him. My address? You better be bloody joking, son.' And he slammed the phone down.

As an earthquake of music began to throb from the roof, he muttered: 'Right.'

Racing up the stairs, two at a time, like a demented thing: 'Sarah! Sarah! What is that awful racket?'

'It's *Encore Une Fois*, Dad.'

'Whatever it is, turn it down. Now!'

Sarah lay on her bed. Wondered, could she risk a toke? Better not, leastways till Mum got home.

'He who hits first gets promoted'

(Detective Sergeant Brant)

Brant leant over the suspect, asked: 'Have you ever had a puck in the throat?'

The suspect, a young white male, didn't know the answer, but he knew the very question boded ill.

Brant put his hand to his forehead said: 'Oh gosh, how unthinking of me. You probably don't know what a puck is. It's my Irish background, those words just hop in any old place. Let me enlighten you.'

The police constable standing by the door of the interview room shifted nervously. Brant knew and ignored him, said: 'A puck is—' and lashed out with his closed fist to the man's Adam's apple. He went over backwards in his chair, clutching his throat. No sound other than the chair hitting.

Brant said: 'That's what it is. A demonstration is worth a hundred words, so my old mum always said – bless her.'

The man writhed on the floor as he fought to catch his breath. The constable made a move forward, said, 'Really, sir, I—'

'Shut the fuck up.' Brant righted the chair, said: 'Take your time son, no hurry, no hurry at all. A few more pucks you'll forget about time completely. But time out, let's have a nice cup o' tea, eh? Whatcha say to a brewski me oul' china?' Brant sat in the chair, took out a crumpled cigarette and lit it, said in a strangled voice: 'Oh Jesus, these boys catch you in the throat – know what I mean?' He took another lethal pull then asked: 'Do you want to tell me why you raped the girl before the tea, or wait till after?'

Before, the man said.

Brant was like a pit-bull. You saw him and the word 'pugnacious' leapt to mind. It fitted. His hair was in galloping recession and what remained was cut to the skull. Dark eyes over a nose that had been broken at least twice. A full, sensual mouth that hinted at gentility if not gentleness. Neither applied. He was 5' 8" and powerfully built. Not from the gym but rather from a smouldering rage. Over a drink he'd admit: 'I was born angry and got worse.'

He'd achieved the rank of detective sergeant through sheer bloody-mindedness. It seemed unlikely he'd progress in the Metropolitan Police. It was anxious to shed its bully-boy image.

Special Branch had wooed him but he'd told them in a memorable memo to 'Get fucked'. It made the Branch love him all the more. He was their kind of rough.

Outside the interview room the constable asked: 'If I might have a word, sir.'

'Make it snappy, boyo.'

'I feel I must protest.'

Brant shot his hand out, grabbing the man's testicles, growled: 'Feel that! Get yourself a set of brass ones boyo, or you'll be patrolling the Peckham Estates.'

Falls approached, said: 'Ah. the hands-on approach.'

'Whatcha want, Falls?'

'Mr Roberts wants you.'

He released the constable, said: 'Don't ever interrupt my interrogation again. Got that, laddie?'

The CA club had no connection to the clothing shop and they certainly didn't advertise. It stood for Certain Age, as in 'women of a' The women were of the age where they were certain what they wanted. And what they wanted was sex.

No frills.

No hassle.

No complications.

Roberts' wife was forty-six. According to the new Hollywood chick-flicks, a woman of forty-six had more hope of being killed by a psychopath than finding a new partner.

Her friend Penelope had shared this gem with her and was now saying: 'Fiona, don't you ever just want to get laid by a hunk and no complications?'

Fiona poured the coffee, laughed nervously. Emboldened, Penny urged: 'Don't you want to know if black guys are bigger?'

'Good Lord, Penny!'

'Course you do, especially when the only prick in your life is a real prick.'

'He's not so bad.'

'He's a pompous bastard. C'mon, it's your birthday, let me treat you to the CA. You'll get laid like you always wanted and it won't even cost you money. It's my treat.'

Fiona had already decided but wanted to be coaxed, even lured, and asked: 'Is it safe?'

'Safe? You want safe, buy a vibrator. C'mon, live it up girl – men do it all the time, we're only catching up.'

Fiona hesitated, then asked: 'And the men, are they young?'

'None over twenty and pecs to die for.'

'OK then – should I bring anything?'

'Your imagination. Let's party!'

Brant didn't knock, just strode into Roberts' office.

'You don't knock?'

'Gee, Guv, I was so keen to answer your summons, I clean forgot.'

'Keen!'

'Aye, keen as mustard, Guv.'

'Don't call me Guv, this isn't *The Sweeney*.'

'And you're no Reagan, eh? Here, I've another McBain for you.'

He tossed a dog-eared book on to the desk. It looked like it had been chewed, laundered and beaten. Roberts didn't touch it, said: 'You found this in the toilet, that's it?'

'It's his best yet. No one does the Police Procedural like Ed.'

Roberts leaned over to see the title. A food stain had obliterated that. At least he hoped it was food. He said: 'You should support the home side, read Bill James, get the humorous take on policing.'

'For humour, sir, I have you – my humour cup over-floweth.'

The relationship twixt R and B always seemed a beat away from beating. You felt like they'd like nothing better than to get down and kick the living shit out of each other. Which had happened. The tension between them was the chemistry that glued. Co-dependency was another word for it.

The phone rang, postponing further needling.

Roberts snapped it and Brant heard: 'What, a lamppost? Where? When? Jesus! Don't friggin touch him. No! Don't cut him down. Keep the press away. Oh shit. We're on our way.' And he put the phone down.

Brant smiled, asked: 'Trouble, Guv?'

'A lynching. In Brixton.'

'You're kidding!'

'Do I look like I'm bloody kidding? And they left a note.'

'What? Like "Back at two"?'

'How the hell do I know? Let's go.'

'Right, Guv.'

'What did I tell you Brant, eh? Did I tell you not to bloody call me that?'

Brant said: 'Don't forget McBain, we'll need all the help we can get.'

Roberts picked it up and, with a fine overhead lob, landed it in the dustbin and said: 'Bingo.'

'Homicide dicks'

By the time Brant and Roberts arrived in Brixton a crowd had already gathered. The yellow police lines were being ignored. Roberts called to a uniformed sergeant, said: 'Get those people back behind the lines.'

'They won't move, sir.'

'Jesus, are you deaf? Make 'em.'

The medical examiner had arrived and was gazing up at the dangling corpse with a look of near admiration.

Roberts asked: 'Whatcha think, doc?'

'Drowning, I'd say.'

Brant laughed out loud and got a dig from Roberts.

The doctor said: 'Unless you've got a ladder handy, I suggest you cut him down.'

Roberts gave a grim smile, turned to Brant, said: 'Your department, I think.'

Brant grunted and summoned two constables. With complete awkwardness and much noise, they lifted him level with the corpse. A loud 'boo' came from the crowd, plus calls of:

'Watch your wallet, mate.'

'Give 'im a kiss, darling.'

'What's your game then?'

When Brant finally got the noose free, the corpse sagged and took him down in a heap atop the constables. More roars from the crowd and a string of obscenities from Brant.

Roberts said: 'I think you've got him, men.'

As Brant struggled to his feet, Roberts asked: 'Any comments?'

'Yeah, the fucker forgot to brush his teeth and I can guarantee he didn't floss.'

The cricket captain was tending his garden when Pandy came by. A local character, he was so called because of the amount of times he'd ridden in a police car. His shout had been: 'It's the police, gis a spin in de pandy.' They did.

Booze hadn't as much turned his brain to mush as let it slowly erode. Norman had always been good to him, with cash, clothes, patience.

When Pandy told the drinking school he knew the famous captain, they'd given him a good kicking. Years of Jack, meths, surgical spirit had bloated his face into a ruin that would have startled Richard Harris.

He said: 'Mornin', Cap!'

'Morning, Pandy. Need anything?'

'I've an urge for the surge, a few bob for a can if you could?' Once, Norman had seen him produce a startling white handkerchief for a crying woman. It was the gentleness, the almost shyness of how he'd offered it. Norman slipped the money over and Pandy, his eyes in a nine-yard stare, said:

'I wasn't always like this, Cap.'

'I know, I know that.'

'Went to AA once, real nice crowd, but the Jack had me then, they said I had to get a sponsor.'

'A what?'

'Sponsor, like a friend, you know, who'd look out for you.'

'And did you get one?'

Pandy gave a huge laugh, said in a cultured voice: 'Whatcha fink, take a wild bloody guess.'

Norman, fearful of further revelations, said: 'I better get on.'

'Cap?'

'Yes?'

'Will… will youse be me sponsor?'

'Ahm…'

'Won't be a pest, Cap, it'll be like before but just so I'd have one. I'd like to be able to say it, just once.'

'Sure, I'd be privileged.'

'Shake.'

And he held out a hand ingrained with dirt beyond redemption. Norman didn't hesitate, he took it.

When Pandy had gone, Norman didn't rush to the kitchen in search of carbolic soap. He continued to work in the garden, his heart a mix of wonder, pain and compassion.

He'd be dead for weeks before his sponsor learnt the news.

> 'You can't just go round killing people, whenever the notion strikes you. It's not feasible.'

Elisha Cook to Lawrence Tierney in
Born to Kill

Kevin, without knowing it, used an Ed McBain title. As he greeted the 'E' crew with 'Hail, hail, the gang's all here.'

He was tripping out, had sampled some crack cocaine and gone into orbit, shouting: 'I can see fucking Indians. And they're all bus conductors.'

He trailed off in a line of giggles. When the crew had taken their first victim, they had also 'confiscated': a) a mountain of dope; b) weapons; c) heavy cash.

Kevin, sampling all these like a vulture on assignment, roared: 'I love LA!'

Albert, worried, had asked: 'Is it dangerous?' Meaning the drugs, and got a nasty clip round the earhole.

'Dope is risky for those who're fucked up to start. See me, it's recreational. like, that's why they call them that.'

'Call them what?'

He dealt Albert another clip and answered: 'Recreational drugs, you moron. What is it, you gone deaf? Listen to that monkey's shit. Wake up fella, it's the nineties ending.'

He set up another line of the white.

*

Patrick Hamilton wrote: 'Those whom God deserted are given a room and a gas fire in Earls Court.'

If homelessness is the final rung of the downward spiral, then a bedsit may be the rehearsal for desperation. In a bedsit in Balham, a man carefully pinned a large poster of the England cricket team to his wall. He stood back and surveyed it, said:

'To you who are about to die – here is my salute.'

And he swallowed deep, then spat at the poster. As the saliva dribbled down the team, he half turned, then in one motion launched a knife with ferocity. It clattered against the wall, didn't hold, fell into the line. He took a wild kick at it, screaming:

'You useless piece of shit.'

The knife had come from *Man of War* magazine. Monthly, it catered for would-be mercenaries, Tories and psychos. Their mail-order section featured all the weapons necessary for a minor bloodbath. The 'throwing knife' was guaranteed to hit and pierce with 'deadly accuracy'. The man dropped to the floor and began his morning regime of harsh exercises, shouted:

'Gimme one hundred, mister.'

As he pumped, the letters on his right arm, burned tattoo-blue against the skin: SHANNON. Not his real name, but the character from Frederick Forsyth's *Dogs of War*. Unlike the fictional character, he didn't smoke, drink, drug. The demons in his mind provided all the stimulation he would ever need. Words hammered through his head as he pounded the floor:

Gimmie a little country or gimmie rock 'n' roll but launch me to Armageddon I will smote the heathers upon the playing fields of Eton and low I will lay their false Gods of sporting legend I will I will I am I am the fucking wrath of the nineties. The new age of devastation.

'Setting a Tone'

Brant and Roberts were sitting in the canteen. Not saying a whole lot. Both had newspapers, both tabloids. None of the *Guardian* liberal pose in here. In his office, Roberts kept the *Telegraph* on top, lest the brass look in.

They were comfortable, at odd times sometimes were. Grunts of approval, decision, amazement. Of course the obligatory male cry had to be uttered periodically to emphasise there were no pooftahs here:

'Fwor, look at the knockers on 'er.'

'See this wanker? He ate the vicar's dog.'

Emboldened by the reassuring bonding of the sports page, Brant put his page down, had a look around, then took out his cigs, asked: 'Mind if I do, Guv?'

Roberts raised his eyebrows, said: 'And what? You'll refrain if I do mind?'

Brant lit up, asked: 'You packed 'em in, Guv. How long now?'

'Five years, four weeks, two days and...' Roberts looked at his watch, '...Nine hours. More or less.'

'Don't miss 'em at all, eh?'

'Never give 'em a moment's thought.'

Brant's chest gave a rumble, phlegm screaming 'OUT' and he said: 'You heard about the new kid. Tome?'

'It's Tone, but what?'

'He answered a mugging call. An old-age pensioner was set upon by four kids. Took his pension. The usual shit. So, along comes the bold Tone, says: 'Why didn't you fight back?'

Roberts laughed out loud, said: 'He never!'

'Straight up, Guv, the old boy says, "I'm eighty-six fugging years old, what am I gonna do, bite then with my false teeth?" Then, Tone asks if he got a description and the old boy says: "Yeah, they were in their teens with baseball caps and them hooded tops, like half a million other young thugs. But they used offensive language. Might that be a clue?"'

Roberts went and got some more tea and two chocolate snack biscuits.

Brant said: 'Don't wanna be funny, Guv, but I'd prefer coffee.'

'Who can tell the difference? So, are you going to watch out for young Tone?'

'You think I should?'

'Yes. Yes I do.'

'All righty then, we'll make a fascist of him yet.'

'That I don't doubt.'

> 'The King of thieves has come,
> call it stealing if you will but I
> say, it's justice done. You have
> had your way, The Ragged
> Army's calling time.'

Johnny Lamb

After Brant had left Roberts returned to his paper. He wanted to read an interview with John Malkovich. He'd seen him give Clint Eastwood the run around in the late night movie, *In the Line of Duty*.

And here's what he read:

"'What the public perceives is shit and what they think is vomit for the best part. The public doesn't read Faulkner, it reads Danielle Steele. The movies they think are good I couldn't even watch.' – actor John Malkovich."

'Good Lord', said Roberts, 'The man has the soul of a copper, pure brass.' There was a photo of the actor, shaved skull, predatory eyes, and Roberts thought: 'You ugly bastard.' Yet, as is the way of a loaded world, woman adored him. Unconsciously, Roberts' hand ran over his head. The gesture brought no comfort. He remembered when he first courted Fiona – the sheer adrenaline rush of just being in her presence. He missed two people: a) the girl she was; b) the person she'd made him feel he might have been. A deep sigh escaped him.

*

Back at the station, Roberts was summoned to the Chief Super's office. Chief Superintendent Brown resembled a poor man's Neil Kinnock. For a time he'd cultivated the image but as the winds of political change blew, and blew cold, he'd tried to bury it. His thinning black hair was dyed – and very badly. Men believe they can pop into Boots, buy the gear and do the job at home: presto! A fresh colour of youth and no one the wiser. Oh boy, even the postman knows. Women go to a salon, pay the odds and get it done professionally. The Chief's latest colour was darker than a Tory soul. Roberts knocked, heard: 'Enter.' Thought: 'Wanker.'

Brown was gazing at his framed photos of famous batsmen, said: 'Time-wasting by batsmen – like to explain that to me, laddie?'

'Excuse me?'

'Very well, I'll tell you: other than in exceptional circumstances, the batsman should always be ready to strike when the bowler is ready to start his run.'

Then he waited. Roberts wasn't sure if he required an 'Oh, well done, sir!' or not. He settled for not.

Brown ummed and ah'd, then said: 'The newspaper chappies have been on to me.'

'About the hanging?'

'What hanging?'

Roberts explained and Brown shouted: 'Hard not to approve eh, but hardly pc.'

'No. I'm referring to some crackpot called the Umpire, who's threatened to kill the cricket team.'

Roberts smiled, said: 'Then the bugger will have to stand in line.'

Brown gave him the Kinnock look, all insulted dignity.

'Really, Chief Inspector, that's in appalling bad taste. Probably some nut-case, eh?'

'Or a paki more like.'

'Get on it, Roberts, toot-sweet.'

Outside, Roberts muttered: 'get on bloody what?'

*

Brant was mid-joke: 'So I asked her, can I have the last dance. She said: "You're having it, mate."'

Loud guffaws from the assembled constabulary. Roberts barked: 'Get me the current file on nutters.'

As he strode past, Brant clicked his heels and gave a crisp Hitler salute. More guffaws.

The CA Club was situated in Lower Belgravia. Vice thrives best in the centre. Ask Mark Thatcher. Inside it looked like a Heals catalogue. All soft furnishings, pastel colours. A woman approached Penny and Fiona. Dressed in what used to be optimistically called a 'pants suit', she was a healthy sixty. Everything had been lifted but was holding. It gave her face the immobile rictus of a death mask. She gushed:

'My dears, welcome to Cora's. To the CA.'

Penny handed her a card, which she discreetly put away before suggesting: 'Drinkees?'

Fiona had an overpowering urge to shout: 'Get real.' Being married to a policeman did that. Penny said: 'Pina Coladas.'

'Oh dear, yes. Bravo.' And she took off. Fiona said: 'Where is everybody?'

'Fucking.'

Cora reappeared, followed by two young men. They looked like Boyzone wannabies. Cora placed the drinks on a table with a catalogue, said:

'Enjoy, mon cheries.'

The men stood smiling. Fiona looked at Penny, said: 'Oh God, I hope they're not going to sing.'

Penny was flicking through the catalogues. Page on page of guys, all nationalities and all young.

Fiona lifted her drink, said: 'I never know, do you eat or drink these?'

Penny said to the men: 'I'd like to book Sandy,' then nudged Fiona: 'C'mon girl. Pick.'

Fiona tried to concentrate. An entry looked like this:

Photo (some gorgeous hunk)
Name:
Vital Stats:
Age: (all 19/20)
Hobbies: (they all hang-glided, skied and squashed)

Fiona had a vision of the sky over Westminster, near black with gliding Sandys and all with the killer smile. She said: 'Jeez, I can't decide, I mean… are they real?'

Penny, impatient, said: 'I'm getting itchy, twitchy, and bitchy – here, take Jason, he's a good hors d'oeuvre.'

'Will I have to talk to him?'

Penny touched her hand: 'Honey, we ain't here to talk.'

Basic survival: 'Never trust anyone who puts Very before Beautiful'

Phyl Kennedy

The England wicket-keeper, Anthony Heaton, was a rarity in sport. A classical scholar, he believed he had the ear of the common people. In private moments, he'd listen to 'Working Class Hero' and smile smugly.

As part of his public bonding, he frequently rode the tube. But the Northern Line will test the very best of men. As he headed down the non-functional Oval escalator, he whispered:

'*Rudis indegestaque moles*' – 'I'd hoped for something better.'

On the platform, he watched a nun pacing. Steeped in the mystique of *Brideshead Revisited*, he was fascinated by Catholicism. At college he had been described as 'Anthony Blythe with focus'. He thought their rituals very beautiful. Now the nun made a second sweep of the platform, not glancing at the destinations board, which read:

Morden 3 min   Kennington 4 min

Then he saw what she was casing, the chocolate machine. Anthony could quote: 'Oh sweet temptation' and 'Thrice you shall betray me'.

Now the nun stopped and rooted in her habit, her face

flushed with expectation. Coins were 'thunked' in and a calculated selection made. Cadbury's Turkish Delight. A classic. The handle was pulled and the nun moved in for the kill. Anthony watched her face, 'un-lined, unblemished'. She could be sixteen or sixty. Definitely from the Philippines, who were producing a bumper crop of nuns for the nineties.

One of Anthony's team-mates had said recently: 'Hell is Imelda Marcos singing "Amazing Grace".'

No chocolate: *nada*, zip, *tipota*. The nun looked round in dismay. As the Americans say: 'Who you gonna call?'

The train could be heard approaching and Anthony could see tears in the nun's eyes. He moved with the grace he kept for Lords, and one, two, open-palmed he hit the machine.

The Turkish Delight popped out. With a flourish, he presented her with her prize. The nun was beaming, her face aglow, and she said: 'God be praised.'

He nodded gravely, added: 'Veritas.'

After Anthony Heaton's murder, the nun would gaze at his photo in the paper and hope they'd given him the last rites. In her breviary, beside his snap, was a neatly folded chocolate wrapper, smooth as a silent prayer.

David Eddings was one of the England batsmen. He was having a bad morning. His wife had issued an ultimatum.

'You go on tour and I'm history.'

He hadn't handled it well, his reply being: 'I'll help you pack.'

The toaster had short-circuited and there was no bloody orange. Losing it, he shouted: 'Where's my juice?'

From upstairs the sound of slamming doors, suitcases, and: 'That's what the *Daily Express* asked too.'

Said paper had been sniping at his age. The doorbell rang and he shouted again: 'Are you going to get that?'

'Well I doubt it will answer itself, darling.'

A hiss underlined the endearment. A yeah, he'd definitely heard a sss... Striding to the door, muttering: 'This flaming better be good.'

He pulled it open. A postman, not their usual. Postbag held in front of his chest, he said: 'Batsman leaving the field.'

'What?'

And coming out of the bag was a barrel of a gun. Now the postman intoned: 'I am the Umpire. When a batsman has left the field or retired and is unable to return owing to illness or injury, he is to be recorded as "retired, not out".'

And he shot David Eddings in the face.

Weights...

Whes the call on the shooting came through, Brant was, as usual, missing. He'd left his bleeper on the desk. There it shrilled till a passing sergeant dropped it in the bin.

Brant was in the canteen, smoking a Player's Weight. These were only available in a tobacconist off Bond Street, on a shelf with Sobranies, Woodbines and snuff: the forgotten stimulants of a Jack the Ripper-era London. Brant had an arrangement with the owner – 'I'll keep an eye on the premises.' There had been five break-ins since his pledge. Unfazed, he asked: 'Did they get my Weights?'

'No.'

'See: no taste, no worries.'

He took a deep drag now. As the powerful nicotine blasted across his lungs, he gasped: 'Jaysus.'

A radio was blaring Michael Bolton and he muttered: 'Shut up, yah whining wanker – put a bloody sock in it.' And chanced another draw of the cigarette. In unison, if not in harmony, a WPC gave a series of short, sharp coughs. Brant's head came up like a setter.

'Hello,' he said.

'S-sorry sarge, the WPC stammered, 'I've got a strep throat – nothing will shift it.'

He gave a professional smile. It's in the manual and has absolutely no relation to warmth. He said: 'There is one sure cure.'

The WPC was surprised. New to the force, she'd heard he was an animal but maybe she'd be the very person to bring out his feminine side. Show he was gentle, caring and compassionate and hey – he wasn't at all bad looking – a bit rough but she could change that. Encouraged, she asked: 'What's it called?'

'C-men.'

'C-what?'

'C-men. It's got to be delivered orally. I'm off at four, I could come round, let you have it.'

A moment before it clicked. As the words took shape on her lips, she felt bile in her stomach. Jumping to her feet she said: 'You… animal!' And ran out, leaving three-quarters of her apple danish. He reached over, broke a wedge off and popped it in his mouth, went 'mmm,' and muttered: 'Women? Go figure.'

The duty sergeant put his head round the door and said: 'Brant, all hell's broken loose, better get outta here.'

'Another hanging, I hope.' He snatched up the remains of the danish and between bites managed to hum a bar of Michael Bolton.

The fucking rooms at the CA were a rampage of luxury: Wet bar, silk sheets, soft to softest furnishings. Jason was twelve, or so it seemed to Fiona. But the body was a healthy twentysomething. He'd lightly oiled his torso and it made his tan glow. He was dressed only in black shiny briefs. Fiona couldn't keep her eyes off it. She had a variety of witty lines to break the ice but they translated as 'ah.' Jason smiled – teeth that shouted 'capped glory'. He said: 'What's your pleasure?'

Alas, he tried for husky, but Peckham and tight undies played havoc. Fiona went up to him, said: 'Shush. Shh…' She put her hand in his knickers, gasped: 'Oh God!', fell to her knees and took him in her mouth. Then, breaking off, she said: 'Jason, I want you to fuck me till I can't walk but I don't want you to speak, not now – not ever. Can you do that?'

He could and he did.

Her husband, meanwhile, was also being fucked, but over, by the Chief Super, the press and Mrs David Eddings.

By the time Brant reached him, he was in the coronary zone, barked: 'Been on vacation, have you?'

'Sorry, Guv, was chasing down leads on the "E".'

'The what?'

'"E", sir – E for enough. The hanging job, or did it slip your mind? You've a lot on, I suppose.'

Through a barrage of obscenities, Roberts outlined the cricket murder. Brant looked thoughtful, then said: 'Bit of a sticky wicket what?'

'You know cricket?'

'That's it, Guv – only the one expression, I have to ration it.'

'Well, you're about to get an education. I shall personally ensure you get a crash course. Don't the Irish play?'

Brant tried to look deprived. It made him satanic.

'Just hurling I'm afraid.'

'What's that then?'

'A cross between hockey and murder.'

'Wonderful, I've a thick Paddy to help me. Get down to the incident room, it should be set up by now.'

'And... er, where's that, Guv?'

'How the bloody hell do I know. Ask a policeman. If you can find one.'

'Righty ho... I'm on it, fret not. McBain has me wise to procedural.'

'Fuck McBain.'

'As you wish, Guv.'

Doggone!

The Umpire had returned to Balham. Back and forth across his bedsit he roared: 'Yes yes yes – we have begun!' and punched the air. The gun was held tightly in his left hand. An impulse to blast holes in the wall was near overwhelming. He marched to the poster of the England team, stabbed his finger in Dave Edding's face, asked: 'Were you surprised, Batman? Were you fuckin' stunned?'

Looking around he found the knife on the floor and began to gouge out the face in the picture. Then he stood back, examined his handiwork, and in a singsong voice, trilled:

'Eeny meeny miney mo

Catch a cricketer by the toe,

If he repents, let him go

Or else the Umpire cuts him so.'

He went to his bed and from underneath pulled a battered suitcase. Opening it he leafed through yellowing newspaper. Fragments of headlines registered briefly:

- SCHOOLBOY CRICKET SENSATION
- YOUNGEST EVER INTERNATIONAL
- BITTER END TO SCHOOLBOY'S DREAM

He threw his head back and emitted a long cry of pure anguish. Unknowing, he shredded the frail papers as he lamented. Pieces of the articles fluttered briefly round his legs then settled in a mess about him. It appeared as if he'd been marooned in the remnants of an old wedding. The party had moved on but he'd become lost in the primary celebration. Not that he wouldn't get to the feast; it was more… he didn't *realise* he could have moved on.

*

WPC Falls, by one of those meaningless coincidences, also lived in Balham. Not in a bedsit though. The house had been left to her by her mother. Her father, a perpetual drunk, made hazard raids on her time and decency. Both were running thin.

She'd had a long day. It seemed a convention of lunatics had invaded their manor.

Vigilantes, cricket executioners, and God only knew how many copycats plus false confessors. She went to the hi-fi, put the Cowboy Junkies on loud. *The Trinity Session* had been literally worn out. Now she was wearing out the Canadian live album. As she ran a bath, Mango Tameness' enchanting voice began: 'The song's about a fucked-up world, but hey – a girl ain't givin' in.' *Oprah* material, but when Mango sang it, just maybe there was a chance. In a weak moment she'd told a cop about her passion for the group. True to form, he zeroed in on prejudice: 'Junkies! You're listening to bloody dopers. Try Coldharbour Lane or Railton Road on Friday night.'

And he'd ranted till she lied and said Dire Straits were what got her hot. It blew him off.

Now as she sank into the bath, Mango was telling of the hunted. Out loud Falls said: 'Sing it, sister.'

The immediacy of the day began to fade. She'd had a call to a tower block near the Oval. Surname Point: the top of the building had come off in a big storm that snuck past Michael Fish – 'no storm tonight,' he forecasted, as the worst one in a hundred years came thundering down the pike. The call was to the thirteenth floor. Did the lifts work? Not that time. An irritated Falls finally made it to the scene. A crowd was gathered outside an open door. A huge black woman approached, asked: 'Couldn't they send a bloke then?'

'I'm it.'

'Should've sent a fella.'

'Can we get to it?'

'Blimey… 'ere look, they've sent a woman!'

And a chorus of 'Should've been a bloke' rose from the assembled. Out of patience, Falls snapped: 'What's the bloody problem?'

''Ere, don't you get shifty with me, sis… blokes don't get like that.'

Falls forced her way through the crowd. Someone goosed her but she had to let it go. She strongly suspected the black woman.

A neighbour's dog had been a constant barker. Open all hours. Now the occupant, a white male in his fifties, had snatched the animal and was holding it over the balcony.

Falls had eventually elicited his name: 'Mr Prentiss. You don't want to do this.'

'Oh yes I do.'

The assembly pitches in: 'Drop the fucker, see if he bloody flies. Go on then, let 'im go.'

Falls shouted: 'Be quiet!'

And was answered by: 'Show us yer knickers.' And quieter observations, such as: 'She's got the hump – throw her off 'n' all.'

Now Prentiss spoke again: 'See, he's not barking now. See? First time in six months he's bloody shut it.'

Falls had taken Psychology One and had done some classes in hostage negotiation. But not enough. She said: 'We can work this out.'

'Bollocks.' And he let the dog go. The animal got in one last bark on his descent.

After Falls had marched Prentiss down the stairs, all thirteen stories, someone said: 'You know what I fink, love?'

'Yeah, yeah. They should have sent a bloke.'

'No, you should've took the lift – it come back on while you were on the balcony.'

Prentiss, wiping sweat from his face, said: 'You sure you're in the right career, darlin'?'

Falls was too knackered to reply.

Hand job

When Roberts got to his home it was clocking midnight and he was clocking zero.

The house was in Dulwich, the Knightsbridge of south-east London. This was always said with a straight face. Else how could you say it? Dulwichians liked to think they were but temporarily out of geographic whack. Others said out of their tree. Dulwichians felt they gave the rest of the south-east something to aspire to. And they did. The aspiration to break into their homes and hopefully kick the shit outta them as bonus.

Hope is the drug. The mortgage was the payment from hell and Roberts carried it badly. In the sitting room, he sank into a leather chair that was designed for show. You moved – it cracked and ran friction on the arse. Course it cost a bundle, which was why he felt obliged to use it. Fiona Roberts wasn't long home but she showered, put on a worn housecoat and hoped she looked... well, housewifey. Jason had done as instructed and she could hardly walk. Composing herself, she got the expression fixed, the bored look of feigned interest. Looking as if she couldn't quite remember his name and jeez, how much did she care? All this went right out the window when he said:

'You look shagged.'

Guilt cascaded over her and she floundered, tried: 'What a thing to say to your wife, good Lord!'

But he wasn't even looking at her now, asked: 'Pour us a scotch, love – I'm too whacked to wank.'

Indignation rose, as did her voice: 'How dare you use such language.'

'What? What did I say?'

'That you're too tired to to masturbate.'

He laughed out loud, said: 'Jeez, get a grip. *Wag*, I said, too tired to wag. You've bloody sex on the brain.'

She sloshed whisky into a tumbler and pushed it to him. He said: 'Thanks dear, so kind – like to hear about my day?'

'I'm rather tired. If it's all the same to you, I'll turn in. Good night.' And she was outta there. For a few moments he just sat, the whisky untouched in his hand. Then he chanced a large sip, let it settle and said: 'A hand job would have been nice.'

On his way home Brant stopped at an off-licence and picked up half a dozen Specials. The owner knew him and, not with affection, asked: 'You want them on the slate, Mr Brant?'

Brant gave his malevolent smile, tapped his pockets, said: 'I find myself without the readies, Mr Patel. Wanna take a cheque?'

They both had an insecure chuckle at the ludicrousness of such a gesture. As if on afterthought, Brant said: 'Chuck some readies in there, I'll get back to you on Friday – how would that be?'

Patel turned to the cash register, raised his eyes to heaven and rang no sale. The continuing story with Brant, who'd planned it for his tombstone. Patel handed over the carrier bag: 'A pony all right, Mr Brant?'

'Lovely job and you're a lovely fella. No further trouble with the NF, I trust?'

'No, Mr Brant, all is rosy.'

Brant nodded and turned to go, then: 'By Jove Patel, I must say you've mastered the Queen's tongue rather well, eh? They'd be impressed back in Calcutta.'

Patel couldn't quite let it go, said: 'Mr Brant, Calcutta is in India. I am from Rawalpindi.'

'Whatever.' And he let his eyes flick across the price list, adding: 'Thing is boyo, you keep charging like that you'll be able to bring the cousins over from both places eh? You keep it in yer pants now, hear?'

After he'd gone Patel slammed the counter in frustration. He considered again making the call to Scotland Yard.

Brant lived in a council flat in Kennington. On the third floor, it was a one-bedroom basic unit. He kept it tidy in case he scored. One marriage behind him, he was out to nail anything that moved. Roberts' wife was his current obsession. As a trophy fuck she couldn't be bettered. Plus, as he said: 'A pair of knockers on her like gazooms.'

One wall was devoted entirely to books. All of Ed McBain, the 87th Precinct stories. Two shelves were given to the Matthew Hope series – a less successful enterprise for the said writer. The lower shelf was Evan Hunter, including *The Blackboard Jungle*.

Brant liked to think he had thus the three faces of the author. The 87th's went all the way back to the original Penguin editions. Brant kicked off his shoes, opened a Special and drank deep, gasped: 'Bloody lovely, worth every penny.' He settled in an armchair and begun to muse on a White Arrest. First he picked up the phone – get the priorities right.

'Yo, Pizza Express, account number 936. Yeah, that's it, bring me the pepperoni special. Sure, family size.' And then he thought – go for it, do the line they use in every movie: 'And hold the anchovies. Sure, before Tuesday. OK.'

Back to his musing. There were no two ways about it:

One: Roberts was fucked. Two: The station was fucked and he was poised to be the worst fucked of all. All his little perks, minor scams, interrogation techniques, his attitude, guaranteed he'd be shafted before the year was out. A grand sweep of the Met was coming and they were top of the list. Unless… Unless they pulled off the big one, the legendary White Arrest that every copper dreamed about. The veritable Oscar, the Nobel Prize of criminology. Like nailing the Yorkshire Ripper or finding shit-head Lucan. It would clear the books, put you on page one, get you on them chat shows. Have Littlejohn kiss yer arse, ah!

He crushed the can in excitement. Jeez, even his missus would want back.

The doorbell went, crushing his fantasy. A young kid with the pizza. He checked his order form: 'Brant, right? Family size pepperoni?'

'That's it, boyo.'

The list was rechecked and then the kid said: 'It's to go on a slab?'

'Slate, son, but hey, I was all ready to pay. However, I will if they insist!'

He took possession of the pizza. 'Oh yeah, you deserve a tip don't you?'

'If you wish, mister.'

'Don't do it without condoms.'

And he shut the door, waited. Moments later, a half-hearted kick hit the door. He was delighted. 'Good lad, that's the spirit – now clear off before I put my boot in yer hole.'

After eating most of the meal, he had to open his trousers to breathe and could hardly get the beer down. He hit the remote just in time for *The Simpsons*. Later he'd catch *Beavis and Butthead*. He thought: 'Top of the world, Ma.'

> 'All of us that started
> the game with a crooked
> cue... that wanted so much
> and got so little that
> meant so good and did so
> bad. All of us.'

> Jim Thompson

Jacko Mary was living proof of the adage 'Never trust a man with two first names.' He was a snitch. Not a very good one. But the vast machinery of policing needs a few key ingredients:

a) Ignorance, b) Complicity, c) Poor wages, d) Snitches.

Or so the received wisdom goes. He was what the Americans call 'of challenged stature'. He was short. And he fuckin' hated that. Roberts met him at the Hole in the Wall at Waterloo. The very walls here testified to serious, no-shit drinking. A toasted sandwich and a milk stout on the table before Jacko. He said: 'Afternoon, Guv.'

'Whatever.'

'You want anything, Guv?'

'Information.'

Jacko looked hurt, said: 'Can't we be civil?'

'You're a snitch, I'm a policemen, ain't no civility there.' Roberts spoke more harshly than he felt, as he had affection for Jacko, not a huge liking, but in the ballpark. The snitch seemed different but Roberts couldn't quite identify the reason, then he noticed a badge on his coat, two ribbons intertwined, one gold one pink.

'What's that?'

'Oh, it's for people who've had cancer.'

Too late, Roberts realised what was different. Jacko was renowned for his head of jet black hair. So dark it looked dyed. Now huge clumps were missing and Roberts wondered if he was losing his grip. Now he didn't know what to say, said: 'I dunno what to say.'

Jacko touched the top of his head. 'It's coming out in clumps. Every time I comb it there's more on the bleeding brush than on the head. It's the chemo what does it.'

'Ahm… lemmie get you a drink.'

'Naw, won't help me hair. The doctors say it's non-invasive, know what it means?'

'I don't.'

'Not spreading. It's a nice expression, though, don't you fink? Like cancer with a bit o' manners.'

Roberts wanted to go, screw the chance of information, but he felt he should at least make an effort. So he said: 'Don't suppose you can tell me where to find the lunatic who's wasting the cricket team?'

'Naw, don't really do nutters. Mind you, there's two crazy brothers in Brixton might be worth a roust.'

'Who are they, then?'

'The Lee brothers, Kevin and Albert. Word on the street is they've come into heavy action.'

Roberts tried not to scoff. But a note of condescension crept into his voice. 'Small time, Jacko. I know their form. Strictly nickel and dime.'

'I dunno Guv, there's—'

But Roberts cut him off. 'Sorry Jacko, when you've been at this game as long as I have, you develop a nose.'

Then he rooted in his jacket and produced a few notes, apologising: 'It's a bit short, Jacko.'

Jacko Mary gave a huge laugh. 'You're talking to me about short?'

Clue like

Penny was losing it. Tried not to scream at Fiona Roberts as she asked: 'You're saying you won't come to the CA with me?'

'Not today Pen, I'm up to my eyes.'

'I need you, Fiona.'

'I can't, honestly. Let me call you tomorrow, we'll arrange coffee.'

'Jeez, I can't wait. Thanks a bunch, girlfriend!'

And she slammed the phone down and thought: I could hate that cow. Well, OK then, I'll go shoplifting.'

Thing was, she was a very bad shoplifter. But if she resented Fiona, she out-and-out loathed Jane Fonda. She had admired Jane as the American Bardot and heavily envied her. Then she'd held her breath during the hard Jane bit. Had been in awe during the years of 'serious' actress. Had the hots for her when she was fit and forty. Began to resent a tad how fabulous she was at fifty. Screamed 'bitch' when she sold out at sixty to a billionaire and became one more trophy wife in the Trump tradition.

Penny had been in Hatchards of Piccadilly when a hot flash hit and she'd fled in search of cool air. Outside the Trocadero, she realised she'd stolen a book. There was Jane on the cover. A cookbook. Oh shame! And worse. She hadn't even written it but borrowed recipes from her THREE chefs. THREE! Count 'em and weep. She'd slung the book at a *Big Issue* vendor. The man had taken it well, shouted: 'Saw the movie.'

Restless, irritated, pacing, she tried to watch breakfast TV.

A gaggle of gorgeous blonde bimbos were discussing the merits of being 'childfree'.

'Hold the bloody phones,' she screeched. 'When did we go from being childless to this hip shit?'

A child, the woe of her aching heart and the biological clock hadn't so much stopped as simply run into nothingness.

Upstairs she had a wardrobe full of baby clothes. These weren't stolen. She'd bought each item slow and pained, and paid a lot of money.

'E' is not for Ecstasy

In a house on Coldharbour Lane, four men sat round a coffee table. Open cans of Heineken, Fosters and Colt 45 crowded a batch of black and white photos.

Two of the men were brothers, Kevin and Albert. The others were Doug and Fenton. All were white. Kevin said: 'I don't think they take us serious.'

Albert sighed: 'It's early days, and besides, the cricket thing's got priority.'

Doug joined in: 'Yeah, c'mon Kev, who's gonna get the six o'clock news – a batsman or a dope dealer?'

Kevin slammed the table.

'You think this isn't important?'

Fenton got his oar in: 'Take it easy, Kev.'

Kevin rounded on him, slight traces of spittle at the corners of his mouth. 'Was I talking to you Fen? Did I say one fuckin' word to you, mate?'

'I was only—'

'You were only bollocks – this is my plan, my show.'

'You don't tell me shit, mate.'

Fenton knew the danger signs: up ahead was the twilight zone. He shut up. Kevin grabbed a beer, drained it in a large, loud swallow. The others watched his Adam's apple move like a horrible yo-yo. Finished, he flicked the can away, then:

'Now, as I was saying, before I got interrupted, they ain't taking us serious. Think we're just a one-off. I'll show 'em – the next hanging I'll also torch the bastard. Eh? Whatcha fink o' that? Be like a beacon in the Brixton night sky.'

The others thought it was madness. What they said was: 'Good one, Kev – yeah, torch 'em, that'll do it.'

Kevin sifted through the photos. 'Who's next then? Here's an ugly looking bastard – who's he?' Turned over the photo, read out the details: 'Brian Short, twenty-eight years old, dope dealer, rapist, and lives on Railton.'

'Shit, he's practically next door.'

Albert looked at the others, then said: 'Kev, there's a problem.'

'What, he's moved, that's it?'

'No. He's… I mean…'

'What? Spit it out.'

'He's white.'

'He's scum and what's more, he's gonna burn, and tonight.'

'Kev…'

'Don't start whining, go get some petrol – get a lotta petrol.'

Policing, like cricket,
has hard and fast rules.
Play fast, play hard.

Picture this. Brant is seven years old. The Peckham estate he lives on is already turning to shit. A Labour legacy of cheap contemporary housing is exactly that; Brant has been fighting. But he's learning, learning not to cry and NEVER to back down. At home his mother is bathing his cuts and beatings. He doesn't hear her. *Dixon of Dock Green* is on the telly: 'Evening all,' and Brant whispers a reply. *Z Cars* flames the call and ten years later he answers it fully. Through the years he'll wade through *Hill Street Blues* right along with homicide. But they don't give him the rush. His is an English version of the bobby and for some perverse reason he finds that Ed McBain in the police procedural comes closest to the way it should have been. Long after he'd dismissed Dixon as a wanker, his heart still bore the imprint of Dock Green. In Brant's words, television had gone the way of Peckham. Right down the shitter.

Brant was mid-quiz, deliberately misquoting: 'and the herring shall follow the fleet.'

A constable sneered: 'That's too easy – it's that wanker, the kick-boxer Cantona.'

Brant tried not to show his dismay. He'd been sure it was a winner. A clutch of uniforms was gathered round in the canteen. He said: 'OK wise-arse, try this: "Do you care now?"'

The group laughed, shouted: 'De Niro to Wesley Snipes in *The Fan*.'

Free tickets had been left at the station. Brant stood up in disgust. 'You bastards have been studying. It's meant to be off the cuff.'

He marched away resolving never to play again. Near collided with a galloping Roberts who shouted: 'Another one, they've gone and done it again.'

'The Umpire?'

'No, the other lunatics – the lamppost outfit. C'mon, c'mon, let's roll.'

Outside the library in Brixton, the dangling corpse was still smouldering. Brant asked: 'Got a light?'

Roberts gave a deep sigh: 'This will hang us too.'

Brant nudged him, asked: 'Did you read McBain yet?'

'Oh sure, like I've had time for that.'

Unfazed, Brant launched: 'The 87th Precinct, there's two homicide dicks, Monaghan and Monroe. At the murder scenes they crack a graveyard humour. In *Black Horses* the—'

'Shut up! Jeez, are you completely nuts? Anyone know who this victim might be?'

The uniformed sergeant said: 'Brian Short, twenty-eight years old, dope dealer, rapist, lives on Railton Road.'

Both Roberts and Brant gaped, gave a collective 'what?'

The sergeant repeated it. Roberts said: 'Now that's what I call impressive police work. In fact it's miraculous.'

Brant looked at the corpse, asked: 'Fuckin' hell, you can tell all that from here?'

The sergeant indicated the item he held, said: 'It says so here.'

'Here?'

'Yeah, on the back of this photo.'

'Hey, gimme that.' Brant looked at it and smiled.'How did you get his snappy, Sarge?'

'It was pinned to this notice.'

'"E is for EXTREME measures".'

The police had come prepared this time and two ladders were used to bring the body down. The medical examiner arrived, hummed and hawed, then whipped off his glasses and said: 'This was not a boating accident.'

Brant laughed out loud. Roberts said: 'Wanna share the joke fellas or shall I just continue with my thumb up my arse?'

Intriguing as the picture was, Brant decided not to elaborate and said: 'It's from *Jaws*, sir. Richard Dreyfus said it.'

A press photographer grabbed a series of shots before Roberts cried: 'Get him outta here!'

The evening paper ran a full photo of them apparently laughing delightedly over the body. The caption read: WHAT'S THE JOKE, OFFICERS?

And the accompanying article gave them a bollocking of ferocity.Burned them, so to speak.

Loyalty

Durham, a rising CID star, had been sent to Roberts' station to conduct a full assessment. Now, in front of the whole force, he berated WPC Falls, his voice laden with syrup.

'Ladies and Gentleman, we have here a policewoman who demonstrated yesterday how NOT to handle a case. She went alone to a potentially explosive situation, near invoked a riot and did uncalculated harm to community relations.'

His voice was rising progressively as he built to his finale. He knew his punchline would be hilarious and it showed that tough, stern, he was not without humour. Leadership qualities on display, he got ready.

'But worst of all – to quote the poet, 'The dog it was that died.'

Silence. Rattled, he figured the morons didn't get the reference and repeated it. Nope. Nada. Angry, he tore further into Falls and lost it a bit. Murmurs from the ranks finally halted him. A crushed Falls felt the tears blind her, groped her way out of the room. Durham shouted: 'I don't recall dismissing you, WPC.'

To work on an egg

The Umpire raised himself from the floor and stretching, folded away the killer.

Blinked, opened wide his eyes and was SHANNON, not exactly ordinary citizen, but he had done some of the moves. Even psychos have to eat. He showered and then carefully shaved, using a pearl-handled open razor from his dad. In truth, he'd bought it at a car boot sale but now believed the former. With long, slow sweeps he cut the bristles, and as he reached the Adam's apple he paused. The eyes reflected and for a minute the Umpire had control, whispered: 'gut him like.' Then he was gone and Shannon began to whistle. All spruced up, he said: 'let's get booted and suited.'

For breakfast he boiled two eggs and buttered three slices of bread. Then he cut the slices into thin wedges and lined them up neatly: 'Stand easy, men.'

When the eggs were done, he took a felt marker and did this

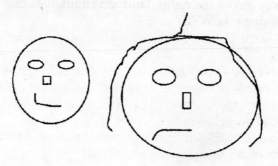

to the eggs. Wrote Jack 'n' Jill on the tips. Ready to nosh down, he sat and crossed himself. He'd seen this on *The Waltons* and felt it was really cool. Evenly, he removed the tops from the eggs, saying: 'Hats off at the table, kids.'

Taking one bread soldier, he dipped it in Jack and ate. To and fro, Jack through Jill, he ate with gusto.

It was DHSS day. Standing quietly in line, Shannon replayed *The Dogs of War* movie in his mind. The window lady looked at his card, said: 'Mr Noble wants to see you – desk number three. Next!'

Shannon waited for two hours before Noble got him. Time for the Umpire to uncoil, begin to flex. Noble had a thin moustache, like a wipe of soot, and he fingered it constantly. With a degree from one of the new polys, Noble had notions. Scanning through the file, he clicked his tongue, said: 'Mr Shannon, we seem to have had you for rather a long time.'

Shannon nodded.

'And... Mmm... you completed the Jobclub, I see.'

Nod.

'No prospects on the horizon – no hopeful leads from there?'

A giggle.

Noble's head came up: 'I said something amusing?'

Shannon spoke, huge merriment bubbling beneath the words: 'I'm seeking a rather specialised position.'

'Oh, and what would that be, Mr Shannon, pray tell?'

The Umpire looked right into Noble's eyes, and the man felt a cold chill hit his very soul.

'I'd like to participate in cricket – a position of influence, ideally.'

And now the laughter burst. A harsh, mocking sound like a knife on glass. Shannon stood up and leaned across the desk, whispered: 'I expect there to be vacancies soon.'

And he was gone.

An ashen Noble sat rigid for several minutes until the tea-lady arrived. 'One or two biccies, Mr N?'

Later in the day, Noble contemplated a call to the police. The loony definitely had a fix on cricket. But what if they laughed at him? It would be round the office in jig-time. Worse, he might have to shave his tash, total horror, resign and sign on. Probably here in his very own domain. A shudder ran through him. No, best leave well enough alone. He'd just put it out of his mind. Right! That's what he'd do. See how decisive he was. Let his 'tache reign supreme.

Falls was twixt laughter and tears, hysteria fomenting. She said: 'You know what the ambulance guy said when he saw how Dad was lying?'

Rosie didn't know, answered: 'I dunno.'

'I do love a man ON a uniform.'

Pause.

Then they cracked up.

BASIC SURVIVAL

'How much more can they not talk to me?'
(d.B)

Kev's brother Albert had a grand passion, the idea fixed almost – the Monkees – as they'd been. And due to syndication, in fifty-eight episodes, they would forever be condemned by celluloid to Monkee around – with shit-eating grins for all eternity. A hell of mammoth proportions, proof indeed that God was deep pissed. To Albert, it was bliss. He knew all the lyrics and worse, lines from the TV series, and horror, repeated them.

When the 'guys', in their fifties and looking old, had a reunion tour, he was appalled. Peter Pan can't grow up, and seeing Davy Jones at fifty-three you knew why. Albert could do the Monkee walk, but had learned the hard way that it's a kink best kept private. When he'd first shown it to Kev, he got a merciless beating. Albert's dream was to visit that beach house where the Monkees had such adventures. When he was nervous, which was often, he'd hum 'Daydream Believer' and believe the fans were fainting outside. The 'E' crew could be like the guys, he thought. He coiled a cog and lit it with a Zippo.

'Hand jobs' Kev called them. He'd go: 'Suckin' on yer hand job. I don't see Mickey Dolenz smokin', eh?'

Not a lot.

In truth, Albert didn't like Mickey all that much. He reminded him of their father and that was the pinnacle of mean. The full down-in-the-gutter vicious bastard. Kev was forever sliding in anti-Monkee propaganda, to rattle the cage. As if he researched it! Like: 'Hey Albert, you dozy fuck, that Mike Nesmith, the one with the nigger hat, he's not hurtin'. His old lady invented Liquid Paper which crafty Mike sold the patent for. Yeah, the old lovable chimp got forty-seven million from Gillette. How about that for bucks, just a carefree guy, eh? No bloody wonder.'

And cloud city when Peter Tork went to jail for drug possession; Kev was delighted. Kept needling. Kept singing:

'We're just goofin' around.'

When *The Simpsons* began to replace the TV show on major networks, Albert hated them double. 'Cos too, they were so ignorant. Homer Simpson was like Kev's role model. Go figure. Albert had been down Brixton Market and – ye gods, hold the phones – he saw Mike Nesmith's woolly hat on a stall, told the stall owner who said: 'Mike who? I don't know the geezer!'

'From the Monkees!'

The guy took a hard look at Albert to see if it was a wind-up, then had a quick scan around, said: 'Yeah, yeah, this is Mike Neville's hat, the actual one.'

Albert got suspicious, said: 'It's Nesmith's?'

'Course it is son, but he uses Neville as a cover. Know what I mean, to avoid the fans like.'

'Oh.'

'Straight up, son. Any road, I couldn't let it go.'

Albert had to have it, pleaded: 'I have to have it.'

'Mmmm. I suppose I could let you have it for twelve.'

'I've only got this, a fiver.'

Which was fast snapped up, with: 'It's yours son, much as I hate to let it go.'

Later, the guy wondered if it was that tea commercial with the chimps, but he didn't remember a hat. As if he gave a fuck anyway. He got out another dozen of them. Kev burnt it the same evening.

To die for

Falls said to Rosie: 'You know how much it's gonna cost to bury Dad?'

'Uh-uh. A lot?'

'Two and a half grand.'

'What? You could get married for that.'

'And that doesn't even include flowers or the vicar's address.'

'You have savings, right? You do have savings?'

'Ahm...'

'Oh Lord, you're skint!'

Falls nodded. Rosie searched for alternatives, then: 'Could you burn him?'

'What?'

'Sorry, I mean, cremate him.'

'He was against that.'

Rosie gave a bitter laugh. 'C'mon girl, I don't think old Arthur has really got a shout in this. He couldn't give a toss what happens now, eh?'

'I can't. I'd feel haunted.'

'Typical. Even in death, men stick to you. What about the Police Benevolent Fund?'

'I've been. They'll cough up part of the dosh, but seeing as he wasn't one of the force...'

Rosie knew another way but didn't wish to open that can of worms. Or worm. She said: 'There is one last resort.'

'Anything. Oh God, Rosie, I just want him planted so I can move on.'

'Brant.'

'Oh no.'

'You're a desperate girl. He does have the readies.'

Then Rosie, to change the subject, patted her new hair-style. It was de rigueur dyke. Brushed severely back, right scraped from her hairline to flourish in a bun. She asked: 'So what do you think of my new style? I know you have to have some face to take such exposure.'

Falls gave it the full glare. She couldn't even say it high-lighted the eyes, a feature that should be deep hid, along with the rest. The eyes were usually a reliable cop-out. To the ugliest dog you could safely say: 'You have lovely eyes.'

Not Rosie.

Falls blurted: 'You have to have some bloody cheek.'

But Rosie took it as a compliment, gushed: 'I'll let you have the address of the salon, they'll see you on short notice.'

Falls wanted to say: 'Saw you coming all right.' But instead: 'That'd be lovely.'

Brant came swaggering in and Rosie said: 'Oh, speak of the devil… Sergeant.'

And over he came, the satanic smile forming: 'Ladies?'

'WPC Falls has a request. I'll leave you to it.'

And she legged it. Brant watched her, then said to Falls: 'What the Jaysus happened to her hair?'

Shannon was in a café on the Walworth Road, not a spit from the old Carter Street Station. He'd ordered a large tea. As it came, an old man asked: 'Is this seat taken?'

'No, sir.'

The man was surprised, manners were as rare as Tories on that patch. He sat down and was about to say so when the young man said: 'No umpire should be changed during a match without the consent of both captains.'

'Eh?'

'Before the toss the umpire shall agree with both captains on any special conditions affecting the conduct of the match.'

'Ah, bit of a cricket buff are you?'

'Before and during a match, the umpires shall ensure that

the conduct of the game and the implements used are strictly in accordance with the laws.'

The old man wondered if he should move but there were no other seats. Plus he was gasping for a brew. He tried: 'Day off work, 'ave you?'

The Umpire smiled, reached over and with his index finger, touched the man's lips, said: 'Time to listen, little man, lest those very lips be removed.'

Before the man could react, the Umpire stood up and came round the table, put his arm over the old man's shoulders, whispered: 'The umpire shall be the sole judge of fair and unfair play.'

The waitress, watching, thought ahh, it's his old dad, isn't that lovely? You just don't see that sort of affection any more. It quite made her day.

As Brant sat with Falls, the canteen radio kicked in, Sting with 'Every Move You Make'. Brant grimaced, said: 'The stalker's anthem.'

Falls listened a bit, said: 'Good Lord, you're right.'

He gave a nod, indicative of nothing. She got antsy, didn't know where to begin, said: 'I dunno where to begin.'

He took out his Weights. Asked: 'D'ya mind?'

'Personally no, but it is a no smoking zone.'

He lit up, said: 'Fuck 'em.' And waited.

Falls wanted to leave. A silent Brant was like a loaded weapon, primed. But she had no alternative. In a small voice, she said: 'I'm in a spot of bother.'

'Money or sex?'

'What?'

'It's always one or the other, always.'

'Oh, right, it's money.'

'How much?'

'Don't you want to know what for?'

'Why, what difference does that make? I'll either give it to you or I won't, a story won't help.'

'It's a lot.'

He waited.

'It's three thou.'

She never knew why she went the extra. Called it nerves, but didn't believe it.

'OK.'

She couldn't believe it, said: 'Just like that?'

'Sure, I'm not a bank, you don't have to bleed.'

'Oh God, that's wonderful, I'm in your debt.'

'Exactly.'

'Excuse me?'

'In my debt, like you said, you owe me.'

'Oh.'

He got up to leave, asked: 'Was there anything else?'

'No.'

'I'll have the money by close of business – that OK with you?'

'Of course. I—'

But he was gone.

Precarious the pose

Brant was in the 'E' room. Expecting a long run. Someone had hooked up a microwave. He looked through the goodies and found a Cornish pasty, muttered 'Mmm,' and put it in the micro. Zapped it twice and had it out. Took an experimental bite and stomped his foot, tears running from his eyes. The pasty, blazing, had fastened to the roof of his mouth. He grabbed a coke bottle and swallowed. Finally the burning eased and he said: 'Jaysus.'

A passing WPC said: 'Don't touch the Cornish, Sarge, they're way past their date.'

The phone rang and he snatched it: 'Incident room "E".'

'Are you investigating the hangings?'

'Yes, that's right.'

'I have some information.'

'Good, that's good. And your name, sir?'

'To prove I'm legit, check the last victim's fingers.'

'Might be a tad difficult, mate – sir.'

'Because of the torching? I doubt that would disguise broken fingers. I'll call back in an hour.' And the caller hung up.

Brant was electric, got on to Roberts and the coroner. When Roberts arrived, he told him of the call and of the coroner's confirmation: 'The bugger was right, and what's more, I've set up for a trace, he was ringing from a mobile, it kept breaking up. We'll have him if he calls back.'

Roberts was impressed, said: 'I'm impressed.'

Brant could feel his adrenaline building. It felt like a hit. Roberts took a seat. A picture of calm, he said: 'Could be the one, the White Arrest.'

Brant had already raced to the same conclusion, was feeling generous in his victory: 'For us both, Guv.'

'No, this is all your own, another Rilke, maybe.'

The phone rang. Brant signalled to the technicians, who gave him the green light, and he picked up: 'Incident room 'E'.'

'You checked the fingers?'

'We're just waiting for confirmation.'

'We're not criminals, we're only doing what the courts are failing to do.'

Roberts made an S motion in the air. Stall.

'Why don't you come in, we'll have a chat, work something out.'

But the caller was on a different track. 'It wasn't meant to be like this, you know, not white people. Not that I'm a racist.'

Brant tried it on. 'Course you're not, I mean you live in Brixton, right?'

Roberts shook his head, signalling U-turn. The caller continued: 'I don't think he'll stop now, he likes it.'

'But you're different, I can tell. I mean why don't you and I have a meet?'

There was static on the line, then a note of panic. 'Shit, I've got to go. I'll call again.'

And then the line died. Brant swore, looked pleadingly to the techs. They were engrossed for a moment, then gave the thumbs up, shouted: 'Got him!'

Brant punched the air: 'Yes!' And a cheer came from the room.

A technician listened, wrote something down, then handed a piece of paper to Brant. He read aloud: '"Leroy Baker". Got yer ass, fucker.' And reached for a phone.

Roberts was up, saying: 'Wait, wait – what's the name?'

'Leroy Baker, we have him.'

Roberts took his arm, pulled him to the other side of the room, saying: 'Listen, Tom.'

'Fuck listen, let's go – we're on him.'

'Tom, the name. It's the first victim.'

'What?'

'Yeah, he's using the guy's mobile.'

Brant sank into a chair, muttering: 'The thieving scum-bag, of all the low-down nasty bastards, I'd like five minutes…' and he trailed off into silence.

The room had gone quiet. Roberts said: 'What's this, you've finished for the day? Get bloody on it!'

A half-hearted hum began to return, with furtive looks to Brant. Roberts touched his shoulder. 'C'mon sergeant, I'm going to buy you a drink.'

Madness more like

Nineteen-sixty-five. The Umpire had been a cricket sensation. As a schoolboy, he'd already been watched by the England selectors. Provision was made to ensure his talent was nurtured and developed. But...

If Albert of the 'E' crew was missing some vital pieces of human connection and born with a lack, then the Umpire was born with an extra dimension – a dimension of destruction. He liked to watch it burn. On the day of his first schoolboy accomplishments, he set fire to the pavilion. And got caught. His father beat him to a pulp and they put him away in a home for the seriously disturbed. They got that right. What they got wrong was releasing him. His first night home, his father took out all the press cuttings. All the stories of hope and triumph, then proceeded to whip him, ranting: 'There'll be no madness in this family.'

Could you beat insanity? It only drives it underground. Teaches the art of stealth. The first time the Umpire burned a dog, he couldn't believe the rush, enhanced by such discovery. In his mind the words were etched: 'See it burn.'

As the years passed, he began to look on the England team. The fame, publicity, accolades he felt were rightly his. It began to foment in his mind: if he couldn't have the prizes, why should they? When he read *Day of The Jackal* he was elated. Then on to *The Dogs of War*, and as his psychosis came to full bloom he imagined himself to be Shannon, the hero of the book. Later, he thought, Frederick Forsyth would base a book on him.

*

Roberts studied the growing pile of paper on the Umpire, said: 'I'll get the murderer sooner or later. It's always simpler when they're insane.'

Brant said: 'That's a hell of a positive attitude. Way to go, Guv.'

A selfconscious Roberts blustered: 'It's a quote.'

'Oh yeah?'

'Thomas Gomez in *Phantom Lady*.'

'Those old movies again, Guv, eh? It's black-and-white, it's a classic.'

'Don't be a daft bugger, sergeant. It's film noir, never better than in the forties and fifties.'

Brant, already losing interest, answered: 'You know, Guv.'

It wasn't that Brant was an ignoramus, Roberts thought, but that he revelled in ignorance. His sole passion was to win. In his mind he played Robert Mitchum talking to Jane Greer in *Out of The Past*:

'That's not the way to play it.'

'Why not?'

''Cause it isn't the way to win.'

'Is there a way to win?'

'Well, there's a way to lose more slowly.'

'Ahhh.'

'Guv. Guv!' Brant's harsh tone cut through his movie.

'What?'

'You're muttering to yourself. Doesn't look good.'

'A privilege of rank.'

Brant was tempted to add: 'Madness, more like.' But he'd tested his cheek enough. For now.

Slag?

Fiona had arranged a 'coffee meet' with Penny, her treat. She'd selected Claridges, to reach for the class she so desperately craved. It would have amused her to learn she shared a musical preference with WPC Falls. As she ordered a double cappuccino with cream, the words of 'Misguided Angel' ran through her head. The waiter was in his twenties and had the essential blend of surliness and servility. In short, a London lad. She admired his ass in the tight black pants and felt a flush creep across her chest. Since Jason, she was drenched in heat. He'd fit perfectly into the CA catalogue. The coffee came with all the prerequisites of the hotel. A mountain of serviettes with the Claridges logo, lest you lost your bearings, a bowl of artery-clogging cream and one slim biscuit in an unopenable wrapper. Penny arrived looking downright dowdy. Not a leg away from a bag lady. They exchanged air kisses. No skin was actually touched. Not so much consciousness of the age of AIDs as the fact that they were steeped in pretension.

Fiona led: 'Are you all right?'

'Don't I look all right?'

'Well, no... no, you don't.'

Penny turned her head, shouted: 'Waiter, espresso before Tuesday, OK?'

Fiona cringed. 'They're not big on shouting in Claridges. Discretion is such a form that they'd really appreciate you not showing at all. But if you must, then quiet, eh?'

Penny took a Silk Cut from her purse, said: 'I'm smoking again, so shoot me.'

The waiter brought the coffee. No perks with this, just the

basic cup and saucer. He waited and Penny snapped: 'Take a hike, Pedro.'

He did. Then, no preamble, she launched: 'The bastard's leaving after twenty-six years of marriage. He's off.'

'But why?'

'He needs space. Can you believe it, that he'd use that line of crap to me? Everyone's in therapy and no one's responsible anymore.'

'You'll have the house?'

'I'll have his balls, that's what I'll have.'

Then she rooted in her handbag, produced a boxed Chanel No. 5 and flung it on the table, said: 'I got you a present.'

'Oh.'

'Sorry it's not wrapped. Well, it's not paid for either.'

'I don't follow.'

'I nicked it. That's what I'm doing these days, roaming the big stores and stealing things I don't even want. On Monday I took a set of pipes. You wouldn't prefer a nice briar, would you?'

'No. Oh, Pen, if you need help—'

'Go into therapy is it? Find my inner child and thrash it?' She jumped up. 'I'll have to go. I'll call you.'

And she was gone. It was a few moments before Fiona realised that Penny had pocketed the espresso cup. She gave a deep sigh, thinking: 'It's nothing to do with me.'

But it was. Penny had a major effect on her life. She opened the Chanel, put a bit behind her ears, said: 'Mmm, that's class.'

The leader of the 'E' crew, Kevin, was singing at the top of his voice: 'Tom Traubert's Blues', aka 'Waltzing Matilda'. He was well pissed, empty Thunderbirds strewn at his feet. As the high point of the song touched crescendo, so did Kev. He was right moved to tears at the strength, nay, the majesty of the voice. For Christmas his brother Albert had given him Rod Stewart's *Greatest Hit Ballads*, and now aloud he roared:

'I love this fuckin' album!' And cranked open another Thunderbird, near drained it in one gulp. He'd followed Rod from the Small Faces all the way through 'Killing of Georgie' parts one and two, and fuck, never mind that Rod was an arrogant arsehole, the fucker could sing like a nicotinized Angel. Now Kev began to dance, to waltz, one two oops three with an imaginary Matilda. She was a combination of all the women he'd never had. Then, as is wont with the booze, it metamorphosed fuckin' bliss to viciousness in the click of a beat. He stumbled and then pushed the dancing partner away, shouting: 'Slag!' Spittle lined his lips as hate fuelled by alcohol propelled him to a dimension where few would wish to be. Kev had done time, hard time. But he'd discovered books and found they provided a brief escape. His all-time hero was Andrew Vachss with the Burke novels. They were Kev's speed, chock full of righteousness brutality, total vengeance. It never occurred to Kev that the very people Burke pursued were Kevin's own. Not that he didn't identify with the pure villains, the twenty-four carat psychos that scared even Burke. Wesley, the monster who signed his suicide note with a threat: 'I don't know where I'm going but they better not send anyone after me.'

Class act. Kev had copied it down, carried it like a prayer of the damned. Damnation was romantic as long as it didn't hurt. When his brother Albert was born, they left something out, some essential connection that kept him two beats behind. Kevin was his brother and bully. The other two crew members were ciphers, their sole purpose being to fill prisons or football stadiums, and they were partial to both. Go in any bookie's after the big race, they're the guys picking up the discarded tickets, the human wallpaper. When God chose the cast, he made them spear carriers. Rage began early in Kev. A series of homes through Borstal to the one where the big boys play. Prison. In Wormwood Scrubs, he was made to bend over by a drug dealer and thus began his lock on their trade. Discovering Burke gave a hint of crusade to his vision and the seeds of vigilantism were sown. The

Michael Winner *Death Wish* series was a revelation. When Bronson eliminated a guy, the audience stood up and cheered. Kev began to see how he could become famous, heroic and use a gun. If he got to settle personal scores, well hell, that was just how the cookie crumbled. The first weapon he got was a replica Colt and he spent hours in front of the mirror striking poses. Mouthing defiance: 'Bend over! You fucking bend over now... Hey, arsehole... Yeah, you!' He got *Taxi Driver* on vid and finally came home. Here was destiny, and in his movie he'd insist George Clooney played him. Get the chicks hot. At times, standing by Brixton tube station, he's see black guys come past in cars whose names he couldn't even pronounce. Rap music pouring from the speakers and arrogance on the breeze. He'd grit his teeth and mutter: 'You're going down, bad-ass.' When he got the crew together, he laid it out as a blend of Robin Hood meets Tarantino and how they'd be front page of the *Sun*. Doug and Fenton didn't care either way and, if it provided cash, why not? Albert did what Kevin said, as always. The 'E' was born and ready to rock 'n' roll.

Band aid

As Brant and Roberts headed for the pub, they passed a urinating wino. Delirium tremens hit him mid-piss and his body did a passable jig. Brant said: 'A river-dancer.'

The pub was police-friendly. Meaning if you were a cop, they were friendly, if you weren't, you got shafted. A blowsy barmaid greeted them: 'Two officers.'

Brant smiled and said: 'My kind of woman.'

'Friendly?' said Roberts.

'No, big tits.'

Roberts ordered two pints of best and Brant added: 'Two chasers, Glenfiddich preferably.'

Roberts said: 'Cheers.'

'Whatever.'

'You know, Tom, we should do this more often.'

'We've never done it before.'

'Oh, are you sure?'

'I'm positive, Guv.'

'Hey, Tom, no need for that here, we're not standing on rank.'

But he did not offer an alternative. Brant sank the short, said to the barmaid: 'Maisie, same again.'

'That's her name?'

'Is now.'

Four drinks passed. Roberts offered: 'You're a single man now.'

'That's me.'

'No kids.'

'None that I've admitted to.'

Six drinks later, Brant's turn: 'You and yer missus, Guv, doing all right?'

'Well, she's doing something, not that she tells me, mind.'

Eight drinks later, Roberts: 'I think I'm pissed.'

'Naw, it's early yet.'

Closing time. Roberts: 'Fancy a curry? I could murder a chapati.'

'Yeah, let's get a carryout. Molly!'

'I thought she was Maisie.'

'Naw, it's Molly, they're always Mollies.'

Midnight.

Sitting outside the pub attempting red hot curry, Brant said: 'D'ya want to kip at my place?'

A passing bobby stopped, said: 'What's all this then?'

It took Roberts a few moments to focus, then he slurred: 'Yer bloody nicked, son.'

When Brant finally got home he was beginning to sober up. A foul taste on his mouth, he blamed it on the early Cornish pasty. He never blamed whisky. His sobriety was sealed when he saw the door of his flat off its hinges. He roared: 'Bastards! Not to me, not ever!'

The living room was destroyed. Ripped and gutted photos. But his beloved book collection: the McBains were shredded, the delicate Penguin covers torn to pieces. Piled on top were remnants of Matthew Hope and Evan Hunters. To cap it, urine had been sprayed all over. Tears blinded him and a sob-whisper: 'Yah fuckin' animals.'

He ran to the bedroom, tried to ignore the used condom on his pillow, went deep into his dirty laundry, extracted a bundle of undies, roared in triumph: 'Ah, yah stupid bastards,' extracted a Browning automatic, fully loaded, shoved it in the waistband of his trousers and stalked out. Left the door as it was, said: 'Daddy's gone a-hunting.'

Brant's shoulder took the door off the basement flat. He felt that was poetic justice at the very least. Inside, the occupant began to rise from bed. But Brant was over and kneeling on his chest within seconds, saying: 'Sorry to disrupt your sleep, Rodney.'

'Mr Brant, oh God. Mr Brant, what's going on?'

'Someone turned my gaff, Rodders, someone very bloody stupid, and by lunch today you'll have their names for me, else I'll move in with you.'

'Your gaff, Mr Brant? No one would have the bottle, unless it were junkies, yes, has to be, they don't know from shit.'

'The names, Rod, by lunchtime. Am I clear?'

He let his full weight settle and Rodders gasped, then managed: 'OK Mr Brant, OK.'

Brant got up, asked: 'Got any aspirin? My head is splittin'.'

As he left, Rodney asked: 'My door, Mr Brant, who's gonna see about that?'

Brant looked at it with apparently huge interest, then said: 'Don't leave it like this, it's a bloody open invitation, know what I mean?'

Rodney rang Brant at 11.50, said: 'I found the geezers who done yer, Guv.'

'Yeah?'

'They're junkies, like I said. A guy and his girlfriend. Yer own crowd as it happens.'

'What, they're coppers you mean?'

Rodney didn't know if this required a polite laugh. Brant's humour was more lethal than his temper. He decided to play it straight, said: 'Ahm, like Micks, you know, Oirish. But they've been here a bit so they speak a mix of Dublin and London.'

'So where do I find these cultural ambassadors?'

'They have a pitch at the Elephant and Castle, in the tunnels there. He sits and she begs.'

'How Job Centre-ish, eh?'

Rodney felt sweat gather on his brow. Any dealings with Brant had this effect. He hoped to terminate the call with:

'They're easily recognisable as they wear a band aid under the left eye.'

'Why?'

'Fuck knows.'

'OK Rodders, you done good. Stay in touch.'

'Definitely.'

And he put the phone down. His heart was whacking in his chest. However bad he felt, he knew it was way beyond what a set of junkies would soon be experiencing. But he shrugged it off, saying: 'For all I know, they're Ben Elton fans.'

Brant found them in jig time. Sure enough they were in the tunnels, begging and band-aided.

Unlikely lad

The man was sitting on a blanket and the woman was pacing. They had the uniform intimidation: combat jackets, Doc Martens and an air of menace. No dog, surprisingly. Brant looked up and down. Nobody about. He kept his head down and walked up to them, giving the London look of cowardly expectation. He saw the woman smile as she moved to block his path, whining: 'Few bob for a cup o' tea, mistah?'

As he drew level, he swung round and smashed his shoe into the man's face, then whirled and ran her into the wall. Checking again for onlookers, he then pushed her down beside the man. A symphony of shocked groans came from them: 'Whatcha do dat for, ya cunt?'

'Ah…'

Brant hunkered down. Grabbed the man by the hair, said: 'What's with the bandages, dudes?'

The man was hurt but still managed to look amazed: 'What?'

'The Band Aids Bros, what's the deal?'

''Cos if I'm cut, she bleeds.'

Brant smiled and lashed out with his open palm into the woman's face, said: 'Hey, pay attention.'

She tried to spit, then asked: 'Whatcha pickin' on us for, mistah? We dun nothing to youse.'

He banged their heads together as a man entered the tunnel. Brant said: 'You turned over a gaff, the wrong one, believe me. Now you have two days to compensate me for the damage, or I am talking major hurt. I'll leave it to you guys to figure out how much it should be. Else… well, I'll come looking for you.'

The man drew level and asked: 'Anything wrong here?'

Brant stood up, said: 'Naw, I'm doing a survey on urban deprivation.'

The man peered at the battered couple, said: 'Good Lord, they're bleeding.'

'Yeah, but see, they have band aids, that should do it.'

As Brant strolled off, he calculated the pair's collective age at about sixty. They had the air of a hundred and sixty. Never-no-mind, he thought. Like all junkies, they'd been dead for years, the news just hadn't reached their fried brains yet.

Shannon watched the cricket story fade from page one to back towards the horoscopes. His story! But unlike the 'E' outfit, he didn't get angry. Time was on his side and he knew how to instantly pull it back. He'd been to military shops on the Strand and quite openly bought a crossbow.

The proprietor had said: 'Alas, I've only three arrows.'

The Umpire smiled, said: 'Then thrice shall I smite them.'

The proprietor couldn't give a toss if he answered in Arabic, said: 'Whatever.' And he put the goods in a M&S bag, warning: 'Careful how you handle 'em,' and pocketed the money.

Now the Umpire dry-tested the bow and found it slack. He tightened and tested for over an hour till it gave a taut *zing*. He couldn't believe how easy it had been to kill his second cricketer. At the very least, he'd expected a uniform on the beat. But zip, *nada*, *tipota*.

When he'd begun his crusade, he found most of the team addresses in the phone book. That strengthened his conviction and zeal. Three of them with south-east London homes. Better and better. The sheer power of the bolts enthralled him. As he saw the wicket-keeper stumble down the steps, he felt exhilaration. But cunning ruled. He quickly put the weapon in the M&S bag and simply walked away. Shannon began to reemerge as the two personalities roared: 'Cry havoc and let loose the dogs of war.'

PC Tone was what used to be called a raw youth. He didn't have acne but it was close. At twenty-three years of age, he looked seventeen. Not a big advantage in south-east London. But he had four O-levels and one A-level. The changing Met looked at exams, not faces. When Brant first clapped eyes on him, he'd said: 'For fucksake.'

Tone worshipped the Sergeant. The rep of violence, rebellion and fecklessness was irresistible. That Brant despised him didn't cool his devotion since Brant seemed to despise everyone. Tone figured if he could attach himself to Brant, he'd learn the real method of policing. Not an easy task, as most times he was told: 'Piss off boy.' Until this morning.

He'd been summoned, so to speak. Brant was in the canteen, wolfing down a glazed doughnut. The only person to have his own drinking vessel, even the brass got plastic cups. His was a large chipped mug with Rambo on the side. A logo read: *I'm a gas.* But the *g* had faded. Brant gave a big smile, particles of sugar in his teeth, said: 'Have a seat, boyo.'

Tone was 6'1" and awkward. Roger McGough might have used him for the PC Plod poems. He had his hair cut short and gelled. His face was made up of regular features and his whole demeanour suggested 'unlikely lad'.

He sat.

Brant gave him a full look, then asked: 'Tea or coffee, boyo?'

'Ahm, tea, I think.'

Brant snorted: 'Well, it won't come to you lad, hop up there and gis a refill, two sugars.'

The canteen lady, named Doris, gave Tone a wink, said: 'Watch 'im.'

When he returned, Brant said: 'Lovely job', and took a gulp, went: 'Jaysus you never stirred it.'

Which was true. Then he took out his Weights, said: 'I'd offer you one but it's a smoke-free zone,' and lit up. Tone tasted his tea. It was like coffee or turpentine or a cunning blend of both. Brant leaned over, asked: 'Do you want to get on, boyo, eh? Are you ambitious?'

'Yes, sir.'

'Good, that's good. I have a little job for you.'

'I'm ready, sir.'

'Course you are, a fine strappin' youth like you. You'll sire legions.'

'Sir?'

'Now, there's two dossers, male and female. In their late twenties. They have their pitch in the Elephant and Castle tunnels. They wear band aids on their faces. I want their names, their squat, who they run with, any previous. Got that?'

'Yes sir.'

'Well, don't hang about lad, get crackin'.'

Tone stood up, perplexed, then: 'But sir… Why? Have they done owt? What's the reason?'

Brant held up a hand, palm outward: 'Whoah, Sherlock, hold yer water. The reason is I asked you – d'ya follow?'

'Yes, sir.'

'That's the job, and oh, Tome…'

'Tone, sir. It's an 'n'.'

'Whatever. Mum's the word, eh?'

When the constable had gone, Brant said, and not quietly: 'Fuckin' maggot.'

Room mate?

A hammering likely to wake the very dead

Falls was dreaming of her father when the hammering began at her door. Awakening, she checked the time, 3.30am, and heard in disbelief: 'Open up, this is the police.'

Throwing on a robe, she went to the door and opened it on the safety chain. Brant.

'What the—?'

'I bring you greetings.'

She could smell the wave of liquor and he looked demented. She said: 'Sergeant, this is hardly an appropriate hour.'

'I need a kip.'

And she figured: 'Pay up time.'

Before she could protest, he said: 'Don't be a cow. I've been turned over. I'll sleep on the couch.'

Reluctantly, she opened the door. He slouched in, muttering: 'McBain, Hunter, all done in.'

'Your friends?'

And he gave what she could only describe as a cackle and said: 'Friends? Yes, yes. I believe they were, and better than most.' He flopped down on the couch, said: 'Jay-sus, I need some sleep. Get the light would you?' And within minutes he was snoring. She got a blanket from her bed and as she put it over him she saw the gun in his waistband. Afraid he'd do damage, she reached for it, only to have her wrist seized. He said: 'Don't handle my weapon.'

As she tried to regain her sleep, she wished: 'Hope he shoots his balls off.'

Falls prided herself on the flat being a 'smoke free zone'. Even her old dad, no matter how pissed, never had the bottle to light his 'home-mades' there. Now she woke to the stench of nicotine, clouds of it hung in the air. Storming out to the living room, she found Brant wrapped in her best towel, a cigarette dangling on his lips. He said: 'Breakfast's made. Well, sort of. I've boiled the water. Whatcha fancy, coffee all right?'

'No thank you, I'm a tea drinker.'

As she went into the kitchen, he observed: 'Jay-sus, you've got a big arse, haven't you?'

The kitchen was a ruin. Used cups, stained teatowels, opened jars left everywhere. He strolled in after her, asked: 'How'd it go then?'

'What?'

'The funeral.'

'Oh. Great. No, I mean OK, it was small.'

'He was a small man, eh?'

She glared at him: 'Is that supposed to be funny?'

'Did Roberts go?'

'Yes, him and Mrs Roberts.'

'Ah, the lovely Fiona. I could ride that.'

She slammed a cup on the sink, said:

'Really, Sergeant. Are you trying to be deliberately offensive?' He gave a look of near-innocence.

'Me? Listen babe, don't get yer knickers in a twist, this is my good side.'

She looked at him with distaste, said: 'Your chin is bleeding.'

He wiped at it with an end of the towel, her favourite white fluffy one, said: 'Them lady razors, near tore the face offa me.'

Another item for the bin, she sighed. He stood up, said: 'I need to ask your... co-operation.'

'Oh?'

'If certain items – shall we say information – about the big cases, arrive, I'd appreciate a nod before it gets to Roberts.'

'I don't know, Sarge, I mean..'

'C'mon Falls. I'm not asking much. He'll be informed. Eventually.' Without another word, he went into the sitting room, dressed, and presented himself, asking: 'How do I look?'

'Er…'

'Yeah, I thought so. I've got to go chat to a junkie.'

She felt she'd been a tad cold, nay harsh, and tried to pull back a bit. In the hall, she said in a soft voice: 'Sarge, thanks for not, you know, trying it on.'

'Hey, I don't jump the help, OK.'

Roberts had watched a documentary on Francis Bacon. He especially liked Bacon's cry when he entered a club in Soho: 'Champagne for my real friends. Real pain for my sham friends'. He was about to experience some major pain himself. The Chief Super was having more than a piece of Roberts' hide and kept repeating: 'I'm not the type to say "I told you so".'

He was crowing over the 'solution' to the cricket murder. Roberts was seething, said quietly: 'Oh, it's been solved?'

'Don't take that tone with me, laddie. It's solved as far as we're concerned.'

Roberts wanted to shout: 'Fuck you, sir, fuck the brass and the chain of command and the politicians.' But he said: 'If you say so, sir.'

'I do say so. Our American cousins talk about bottom feeders. Are you cognizant with it?'

'Bottom of the shit pile, sir, would that be close?'

'Brant, now he's a good example. Look here.' And he threw a document across the desk, said: 'The yard have been on to me. Your precious Detective Sergeant is accused of bribe-taking by a Mr Patel, of intimidation by a tobacconist in the West End, of brutality by an accused rapist, of freebies by a pizza company… the list goes on.'

Roberts barely glanced at it, said: 'Nickel and dime. He's a good copper.'

'He's finished, that's what he is. I doubt even a cream arrest could save him.'

'That's white, sir. A White Arrest.'

'Are you sure? Well, I want to ensure he doesn't pull off one of those. So you're back in charge of the vigilante business. See it's put to bed quickly.'

'Put to bed, sir?'

'Get on with it, and I'll remind you of thin ice yourself, questions have been asked before.'

With that he was dismissed. Outside he ran his finger along the rim of his ear. A passing WPC asked: 'All right, sir, your ear I mean?'

'Oh yeah, I've just had a flea put in it.'

The law of holes: when you're in one, don't dig

All hell erupted at the station as the news of the murder broke. The Super charged down the corridor, barged into Roberts' office, roared: 'You're in for it now, laddy, there's been another one.'

Roberts wanted to say, 'I told you so', but instead came running, said: 'Someone surprise me, tell me Brant is here and reachable.' Nobody surprised him.

The down-scaled 'U' incident room was activated and Roberts was given the details of the killing. He asked: 'Any witnesses?'

'No, sir.'

'The weapon?'

'A crossbow, Guv.'

'Bloody hell. Wait until the press get wind of this.'

Silence.

'What, they're on to it already?'

'Sorry, Guv.'

'Holy shit, we're fucked. So no chance of containment, the ol' damage limitation?'

Many heads shook. Negative all the way.

Roberts sat, said: 'Isn't there any good news?'

Falls tried to lighten the mood, said: 'Well, we've got a shoplifter in an interview room.'

He turned his full gaze to her. He spoke slowly: 'That's some sort of levity, I gather. How about this, WPC! Hop lightly to yer plod feet, go interview them and get out of my bloody sight!'

Roberts had thus made two mistakes. The first was not seeing the shoplifter. The second was alienating the hitherto loyal Falls.

> 'Ashen was the way I felt when shunned by people I had justified. Didn't all that much really warrant grief.'

The Umpire

The Umpire's father had adorned the house with framed portraits of cricket's greatest. A who's-who of the best. He'd point to them and shout: 'You could have been better than any of them, but oh no, you're a namby pamby, a mummy's boy. You'll never hold a light to these, these giants.' Light, a light to light. He looked on it like a mantra of darkness.

His father's pride was a three-year-old setter named Fred Truman. Sleek and arrogant, it ruled with ease. The day of the Umpire's transformation, he recalls it like a vision.

The Dogs of War was showing on BBC1. The screen's image flicking back and forth across Fred Truman as he dozed. The Umpire had removed his father's bat from the glass case and said: 'Here boy, come and get it.' As the dog's head reared, the Umpire batted. He heard the crowds leap to their feet at Lords, the applause crescendoed at the Oval and the dog lay stunned. The Umpire laid the bat beside Fred and doused both with petrol. On the TV Christopher Walker loaded up as the match ignited, the words rose: 'Cry havoc and let loose the dogs of…'

*

Falls sat opposite her, put the file on the table and decided to 'Brant' it. Said: 'Well, Penny or Penelope, which?'

No answer.

'Okey-dokey, let's settle for Penny, shall we?'

No answer.

'You're going to jail, Penny.'

Gasp!

'Oh yes. I see you've been up twice before but got off on probation. Says here you agreed to have therapy. I hate to tell you, it isn't working.'

'I can't. I can't go to prison.'

'I'm afraid so, Pen. The courts are sick of rich middle-aged women wasting their valuable time. You'll do six months in Holloway. The girls there, they'll appreciate a bit o' class. Get yerself a nice lez, knit away the winter.'

Penny began to smile, said: 'Oh, I don't think so, you see, I have something to trade.'

'This isn't the bloody market, we don't barter.'

'Don't be so sure. I need to see someone in authority.' Here she gave extra dimension to the smile as she added: 'I don't think it's really a decision for the indians. Go get the chief, there's a good girl.'

Falls came close to clouting her, and realised that Brant might have the right idea. She rose and left the room, still wondering whether or not to go to Roberts. Two factors determined her next move: one, her anger at Roberts; two, almost colliding with Brant.

He said: 'Whoa, little lady, don't lose yer knickers.'

She told him, watched his face and calculated. He said: 'I'll have a word, shall I? You keep watch outside.'

'Shouldn't I be present?'

'Outta yer league, darlin'. Tell you what though, I could murder a cuppa.' And he opened the door, looked back and said: 'Two sugars, love.'

Brant sat down slowly, his eyes on Penny. She said: 'You're a senior officer?'

He gave the satanic smile, asked in his best south-east London voice: 'Whatcha fink, darlin'?'

'I think you look like a thug.'

'That too! So, honey—'

She snapped. 'Don't you dare call me that. I'm not your honey.'

'Leastways not yet. Whatcha got?'

She got foolish and attempted to slap him. He caught her wrist and with the other hand double palmed her. The marks of his hand ran vivid on her cheeks. He asked: 'Have I got your attention now?'

She nodded.

'Okey-dokey, babe. What's cooking?'

She told him about the CA, about Fiona. The whole shooting match. He listened without interruption until: 'You pay for sex?'

'Yes.'

'Fuck me.'

'Actually, it's to avoid that very possibility that we do pay.'

He liked it, said approvingly: 'Cheeky.' Then: 'Run it all by me again, hon.' She did.

He thought for a while, took out his Weights and absent-mindedly offered her one. She took it and waited for a light. He finally noticed, said: 'Jaysus, do you want me to smoke it for you too?' A knock at the door. Falls peered in, said: 'The Chief Inspector is due this way.'

'Shut the door.' She did.

Brant drew on the last of his cigarette, sucked it till his cheekbones hit his eyes, leaned over close, said: 'Here's the deal. It's not negotiable.'

'When the first side has completed its innings, the other side starts its own. A match may consist of one or two innings by each side. If the match is not played out to a finish, it is regarded as a draw.'

The blues

The funeral for the first cricketer was a massive affair. The coffin was carried by his team mates and they'd donned the blazing whites. Even the Devon Malcolm racism storm was temporarily shelved. David 'Syd' Lawrence had called for Ray Illingworth to be banned from every TV and radio in the country. The former chairman of selectors was alleged to have called the Derbyshire paceman a 'nig-nog'. Officers at Lords prayed the funeral would distract from the whole sordid affair. It did.

A huge police presence blocked off most of south-east London. It was feared the Umpire might try to annihilate the remaining nine in one fell swoop. Sky had obtained exclusive rights and was considering a whole series devoted to dead cricketers. It was rumoured that Sting was composing a song for the occasion, but this was proved to be only scaremongering. It scared a lot of people.

Brant and Roberts were positioned on the roof of St Mark's Cathedral, a tactical position according to the Super.

'Out in the bloody cold,' snapped Roberts.

Brant, lowering his binoculars, said: 'Good view, though. the *Big Issue* is selling nicely.'

'We're out of it Tom, the big boys are running the show. The game is a total media event now. See, we'd be on our arses altogether if they didn't need local background.'

Brant didn't care. The more the investigation built, the less notice he attracted. He asked: 'Think they'll get him?'

'They have as much chance as you do of understanding cricket.'

'I know a bit.'

Roberts opened a thermos, refilled their cups and asked: 'Oh yeah? Who's Allan Donald?'

'Um?'

'Like I thought.'

'Tell us, Guv, go on.'

'The South African paceman offered mega bucks by Warwickshire to break the hundred-wicket barrier.'

'He's good then, is he?'

'Good good? He claimed eighty-nine first class victims for the country in '95. In '96, in a summer off from country cricket, he took a hundred and six wickets to help Rishton retain a League title.'

Roberts' voice had risen and he self-consciously pulled back, said apologetically: 'I get a bit carried away.'

Brant found a sandwich, took a bite and said: 'Don't mean shit to me, Guv.'

Roberts went quiet, watched the funeral halt briefly, and he imagined all went still, a suspended moment when past glories, the sound of bat against ball and the hush of the crowd are recalled.

Brant said: 'At a guess Guv, I'd say you haven't suffered from the Paradise Syndrome.'

'The what?'

'You remember the Eurythmics, thin chick who looked like a faded Bowie and a hippy guy named Dave Stewart. Made fuckin' shitpiles of money, that's yer Paradise Syndrome right there.'

'Lucky sod, I could do with a blast of such depression.'

They watched the huge line of cars and Brant said: 'Me, I'd have to put one song to that funeral.'

'What's that then?'

'"Brothers in Arms", no contest.'

Brant began to scratch at his chest and Roberts watched, then said: 'That's it, you're wearing a Met Vest. I thought you'd got fat.'

They were knife- and bullet-proof items issued to 30,000

officers. Needless to say, they hadn't come cheap and they didn't fit under the regulation shirts. Every officer had an issue of shirts and all of them had to be replaced.

It amused Roberts no end and he slipped into a near-pleasant mood. He reminisced: 'The other night, Tom, when we had a few drinks, it was a bit of an eye opener.'

A now surly Brant tore at the vest, saying: 'Bloody things. What? Oh, the other night, yes, I suppose. Me, though, when I go for a few bevvies, I hope it's going to be a leg opener. I'm never wearing these vests again.'

A TV helicopter hovered above and the cameraman zoomed in on Roberts and Brant. The pilot asked: 'Anything?'

'Naw, just a couple of wankers.'

The discarded Met Vest lay on the roof of the cathedral, like a prayer that wasn't said.

The notice read: *Annual Met Dance. Fancy Dress Preferred. Tickets £10.Buffet & Bar Till Late, '60s Band. All Ranks Expected To Attend.* Roberts was staring at it when Brant came up alongside and said: 'Sixties? Does it mean they've been around since then, which would mean they've got to be knackered.'

'You sure have some odd thought processes, Sergeant. I dunno if that's because yer Irish, a policeman or a weird bastard.'

A light hit Brant's eyes. 'Jeez Guv, I've had a brainwave.'

'Yeah? You know who the Umpire is?'

'Now listen, see that fancy dress? Here's something…' Roberts listened to Brant's idea then exchanged:

'I couldn't… good Lord, sergeant, I mean, they'd think we were taking the piss.'

'Ahm, c'mon Guv, it's a wicked notion, you know it is, it's downright – what's the word you like – Nora?'

'Noir. Yeah, it is a bit, lemme have a think on it.'

'Nice one, Guv. You'll see, it'll be a gas.'

'Mmm.'

Law 42: Unfair Play. The Umpires are the sole judges of fair and unfair play

Nobody listens to Mantovani, I mean, get real. Not even Mantovani listens much anymore. He's been consigned to the fifties rack and labelled miscellaneous.

But Graham Norman did, and all the time. His wife had given up joking about it and his kids just prayed the bastard never made it to CD. As captain of the England cricket team, Graham could indulge his whims.

He'd attended an indifferent public school, but ambition burned like the old values. He had a small talent and an unending thirst for practice, plus he knew how to please, especially the press. Early on, he sought them out, and when his ascent began, he took them along. He took up golf to cash in on his name link with Greg Norman. One of his proudest moments was immortalised in a framed photo of them together, with the caption 'Two greats'.

He glanced round his study and felt near satisfied. For a south-east London boy, he'd come all the way. As the strains of Mantovani reached a feeble peak, his wife peered round the door, said: 'For heaven's sake, turn it down. I declare they'll be playing him at your funeral.'

Words that would all too soon come to taunt and torment her.

*

As Brant left the station, a TV reporter approached.

'DS Brant?'

'Who's askin'?'

'I'm Mulligan, from Channel 5. I've been an admirer since you solved the Rilke case.'

Brant guffawed and the reporter stepped back. His hand behind his back, he signalled the cameraman to roll it.

'I said something funny, DS?'

'Mr Mulligan. No relation to the Gold Cup winner, I suppose?'

'I'd like to ask your views on the cricket killings.'

'No comment, boyo, not my case.'

But off the record, what sort of man do you think is behind this?'

'A nutter. One of those bed wetters. Hey, are you filming?'

'Thank you, Detective Sergeant Brant.'

It aired at prime time and among the viewers was the Umpire. The very next day he began to follow Brant. It wasn't in his plan yet to kill policemen, but his rage was such that he felt compelled. Two days later he was at vigil outside Brant's flat when the sergeant emerged with a very mangy dog on a battered leash.

Watching them, he could see the mutual affection. It looked as if someone had attempted to shear the animal. But even the Umpire could sense they made a pair, odd and bizarre but suited. He knew then how to hurt the policeman. Down the street, the dog's heart leapt as his idol said: 'C'mon Meyer, I think it's saveloy and chips for two, eh? Whatcha fink, extra portions? Yeah, me 'n' all.'

It had happened like this: Brant had parked his car on double yellow lines. A traffic warden materialised out of the sewer. Had the book open, was already writing.

Brant flashed his warrant card, said: 'Get a real job, Adolf.'

As the warden slunk back to his yellow lair, Brant headed for his flat. A howl of pure anguish pierced his skull and he whirled round, muttering: 'Jesus, Mary and Joseph, what is that?'

An alley beside Brant's building seemed to be the source. There as another howl of such pain that he felt the hairs stand up on the back of his neck. He moved faster.

A man with a pick-axe was beating a dog with slow, measured intent. Brant shouted: 'Oi, you!'

The man turned, a smile on his face. Well-dressed in a casual way, a knock-down Armani jacket, subdesigned jeans, Nikes. About fifty, he looked like your friendly uncle. Well, your friendly uncle with a pick-axe handle. He said: 'You want some of this, is that it?'

'Yes please,' said Brant, and pushed him.

The pick-axe handle went high and to the right. Brant flinched, stepped to the left and dealt two rapid power punches to the kidney. That's all she wrote.

Brant bent down, rummaged in the man's jacket, extracted a wallet, flipped it open. Read: 'Swan', looked at the man, then added, 'Sorry, MISTER fuckin' Swan. Says so right here. See me boyo I've a white shirt, but I've a blue collar soul. That means I like dogs.'

As the man's pain eased, his attitude returned and he smirked: 'I'll have the police on you mate.'

'I am the bloody police, and this—' he took a wedge of notes from the wallet '—is for the RSPCA.'

Brant went over to the dog and said gently: 'Can you walk boy?' Clumps of hair had been torn from the creature, and there was a large bald patch. Brant stroked him softly, said: 'You're the spit of Meyer Mayer, as bald as an egg.'

Brant was chewing on a slice of pizza, the rest he'd hand fed to Meyer. He was saying: 'I'm a man in his eens. No, not teens, listen up fella, it's caff-eine, nicot-ine, non-prot-een that's made a man of me. You only need to remember one thing about pizza: bite the delivery boy's ankles. Yeah, like Norman Hunter in his day. There was a card, none of yer

Ryan Giggs preciousness. Or here, Dave Prouse, a London boy. Played Darth Vader. Didn't know that, eh? Want some beer?' Meyer hadn't known, and yes to the drink. He liked how it made him dizzy. And shit, he could bite ankles, would welcome the chance.

Brant, lost in wonder, said: 'Jeez, old Dave didn't know what *Star Wars* was gonna do, so he took a flat fee. Three large. But Alec Guinness, he opted for a percentage, has got over a hundred million so far. Make you bloody howl, eh?'

Silence descended as man and dog chewed, pondering the sheer awfulness of chance.

Outside, the Umpire kept vigil, his mind in flames.

Brant was washing Meyer in the bath, said: 'You're a babe magnet.' He'd heard that walking a dog was a sure way to meet women. You exchange phone numbers over leashes and later you did it over the doggy bowl. The other way was supermarkets. Jeez, even Falls had scored there. So OK, she got a security guard, which was kinda rolling yer own, but what the hell. Who's keeping score? The bath didn't alter Meyer radically. Now he was a clean, balding animal, like a *Time Out* reader. Meyer stared at Brant with a look of 'it ain't gonna work'.

And Brant said: 'Hold the phones buddy, you gotta have magnetism, draw them in with scent,' and blasted Meyer with Old Spice. He could almost hear the Beach Boys' 'Surfin Safari', and began to hum it. Not the easiest tune to solo.

As the smell of spice wafted forth, Brant said: 'Hey, not bad,' and gave himself more than a generous dollop. When they hit the common you could have smelled them coming. If dogs could strut, then Meyer tried. And sure, the women were out en masse, both dogged and dog-less.

Alas, the boyos didn't score. In fact, one woman said: 'You barbarian, ought to be arrested for mistreating that animal.' But Brant took it well, almost waxed philosophical, said: 'Might have over done after-shave a tad.'

Babe-less, they headed for the chip shop. The Umpire clocked their progress. Brant might have noticed but he'd

96

already decided it was best they didn't score. Now he could focus on Fiona Roberts. She might have a dog. She already had a husband.

The eyes of a dog

Brant sat down to his breakfast. He'd prepared a mega pot of tea, a mountain of toast, four sausages, black pudding and a badly fried egg. He'd got a wok from cigarette coupons and used it for everything. All the fry had been blasted together and as he studied the mess, he said: 'Lookin' good!'

The dog sat looking at him. William James once said if you want to know about spirituality, look into a dog's eyes. Alas, William never tried to outrun the Rotweillers in Peckham or stare down the Railton Road pit bulls. What was in the dog's eyes was love and gratitude. This man had saved his sorry ass, he knew that. Now if he could only train him, and eating from the wok direct would be a great beginning. He tried to communicate this to the man.

Brant forked a wedge of sausage and said: 'Tell you something, Meyer. I've had some dogs in this gaff, but you're the first bald one.' In McBain's 87th Precinct mysteries, Meyer Meyer is a Jewish detective with not a hair on his head.

Meyer Meyer was already a little legend in the nick. It was even suggested Brant had gone soft. True, he'd felt enormous emotions he'd thought were tight locked away. But it was fun, he got a buzz out of it. The ribbing and piss-taking didn't bother him. Of course it was held in check, since with Brant you never knew. Even Roberts got wind and asked: 'So, Sarge, what's the story with the Rin-Tin-Tin?'

'Meyer Meyer.'

'What?'

'See, you'd know if you'd read yer McBain. But oh no, not Nora enough, eh?'

'That's *noir*, N-O-I-R!'

'Whatever.'

'Where is it then, I mean during the day?'

'Out, he goes out, but he's always waiting when I get home.'

Roberts was quiet and then added wistfully: 'It must be good to have someone waiting.'

When Brant got home that evening, there was no dog.

Brant was mid pie-man's lunch when Roberts called him. 'Can't it wait Guv, I'm in the middle of me dinner here.'

'No.'

'Ah, shit.'

When they got outside Brant asked: 'Where's the bloody fire then?' Roberts gave him a startled look, then said: 'There's been an… incident, one of your neighbours called in. The uniforms are at the scene.'

When they got there Brant pushed ahead up the stairs. The stench was appalling. What remained of the dog was barely recognisable, smoke still trailing slowly up. Brant turned back, said: 'Ah… Jesus!'

Roberts bundled him outside, got him the car, rummaged in the back, produced a thermos, poured a cup, said: 'Take this.'

'Don't want it.'

'It's brandy.'

'OK.' And he let it down. After a moment, Brant produced his Weights, but the tremor in his hand prevented him lighting.

'Give it 'ere, Tom.' Roberts lit the cigarette in Brant's mouth, then said: 'The dog. I mean your dog… he was covered in a white coat.'

'So?'

'A knee-length white coat. It was singed but not burned.'

'Yeah?'

'Well, like we were meant to see it.'

'Jeez, Guv, so bloody big deal.'

'Tom, it's an umpire's coat.'

A house is not a home

PC Tone was also 'encore une fois-ing'. But like Roberts' daughter, it wasn't doing a whole lot for him. He was determined to be cool. But already, even Oasis were on the slide. Never-no-mind, he put on 'Champagne Supernova' and felt connected. On the door of his flat was a full-length poster of Clare Danes, his ideal woman. He'd first stumbled upon her in the defunct series, *My So-called Life*, and he was lost, smitten, entranced. Her part as Juliet in her first full-length movie sealed his fate. Once being interviewed, she'd admitted to listening to 'Wonderwall', 'Like one hundred times.' And he'd shouted: 'Me too!'

Then he got dressed, imitating the words of Brant: 'Let's rock 'n' *roil*.' Like that.

A pair of tan Farah slacks, tight in the ass and crotch so the babes could ogle. But his courage faltered and he pulled on a Nike long sweat, then a shirt loosely buttoned to highlight the sweat's logo: *No. 1*. All right!

Then a pair of market trainers designer-soiled so he wouldn't appear an asshole, like the new kid on the block or something. Shades of cool. A short denim jacket, black lest he appear obvious. Final touch, the Marlboro Lights in the top right-hand pocket. Looked again in the mirror, said: 'My man,' and headed out. Then sheepishly, he had to return a few minutes later to check the gas was off. Worry and cool didn't blend. Shit, he knew that. If Brant didn't check the gas, he'd say: 'Let it blow.' Tone hadn't reached that plateau of recklessness yet. Deeply suspected he never would.

He went to the Cricketers on Thursday, it was darts night.

Maybe Falls would show and he felt his heart palpitate. A wino waylaid him outside the Oval, whining: 'Gis a pound.'

'I'm the heat, fella.'

'Gis two pounds, Mr Heat.'

Tone checked round, then handed over 70p. The wino, indignant, said: 'What am I supposed to do wif this, yah wanker?'

'Call someone who gives a toss.'

He left near dizzy with the macho-ness, but quickened his pace lest the wino follow.

The pub was jammed. Trade was 'aided and abetted' by the 'blue hour'. A police version of the happy one. Two drinks for the price of a single, drink them blues away. It was working. Tone had to elbow to the bar. Tried in vain to get noticed and served. The staff knew rank and knew he hadn't any. So he could wait.

Till: 'What ya want, son?'

Chief Inspector Roberts.

He wanted a tall shandy to motor his arid mouth. 'A scotch, sir.'

And hey, jig time, he'd got it. Roberts nodded, then said: 'Park it over here, son.'

The blue sea parted to reveal a vacant stool. He climbed on, took a slug of the scotch, thought: 'God!' as it burned. Did it ever. Roberts eyed him, asked: 'Got some new clobber there?'

'Oh no, sir, just old stuff.'

The Farahs were so new they sparkled, and no way would they lighten up that crease. Tone had a horrible thought: would the Guvnor think he was on the take? He asked: 'Is Sergeant Brant about, sir?'

Roberts sighed, signalled the barman, and in a terse voice, told of the Meyer Meyer incident.

'Good grief,' said Tone.

If Roberts thought that cut it, he said nothing. Falls and Rosie brushed past, said: ''Night, Guv.'

He didn't answer. Tone shouted: "Night', and tried not to look after them.

Roberts said: 'She's getting hers, eh?'

Tone prayed, crossed his fingers, then said: 'Rosie?'

'Naw. Falls, some security guard's putting it to her.' Tone died.

In this world, you turn
the other cheek, you get
hit with a wrench.

Brian Donlevy, Impact

Roberts saw the young man's face in tatters. He felt a sense of such loss that he could almost no longer recall what power a yearning could be. He touched the bar, said: 'Whatcha say to a double?'

'Ahm, no, sir, I mean… I thought I might call on Sergeant Brant.'

'Mmm.'

'Just to see if he needed anything.'

'I dunno son, he's a man best left to sort himself.'

Tone got off the stool, said, near defiant: 'All the same, sir.'

'Yeah, well, don't expect a warm welcome.'

After Tone had gone, Roberts thought he should have offered some advice on the woman. But what could he tell him? That everything would be fine? Whatever else things turned out to be, fine was almost never one of them. As he left the bar later, brown-nosers called 'Goodnight'. He neither acknowledged nor quite ignored them. It just didn't matter, not when you'd lost the magic of yearning.

PC Tone was more than a touch apprehensive about calling on Brant, but he composed himself, said: 'How bad can it be?'

He heard the music from the street, as if all the cruising

cars in Brixton had a Rap convention. That loud. That annoying. When he reached Brant's door, the noise was massive, and he thought: it sounds like house. It was.

Earlier, Brant had gone into HMV, said: 'Gimmie all the hits of house.'

The assistant, in ponytail and zeiss bifocals, joked: 'Bit of a rave, eh?'

'Bit o' minding yer own bloody business.'

The assistant, who in kinder days would have gravitated from mellow hippy, was now on job release from DHSS in Clapham. He shut it.

Tone had to hammer at the door till eventually it was flung open. A demented Brant before him. Dressed only in maroon Adidas shorts and trainers, sweat cascading down the grey hair of his chest, he sang: 'C'mon ye Reds.'

Tone asked: 'Are you OK, sir?'

'Whatcha want? See if I've a dog licence? Well cop this, I've no bleeding dog, not never more.'

'Sir, sir, could you lower the music?'

'Whats-a-matter boyo? Not *tone* deaf are yer?' Brant laughed wildly at his joke. Tone was lost, didn't know how to leave or stay, tried: 'We'll get him, sergeant.' And Brant lunged forth, grabbing him by his shirt front, the fabric tearing, and roared: 'Oh will you? Didn't I already ask you to find them Dublin fucks with the band aids. Didn't I?'

'Yes.'

'And did you?'

'Not yet.'

'Ah, you couldn't catch a child's cold. Go on, hoppit, fuck off out of it, ya cissy!'

And slammed the door.

As the young copper crept away, he fingered the ripped clothing, saying: 'Didn't have to do that, cost me a tenner in the market that did.' He wanted to bawl.

He who laughs last usually didn't get the joke

Inside, Brant returned to his evening. He'd busted enough raves to get the gist. You stripped to your shorts, took the E and bopped till you dropped. What Brant had felt was, they didn't feel. No one hurting at all.

And that's what he wanted. Because of the dehydration factor, he'd a line of Evians along the wall, and for lubrication, a bottle of Tequila.

New to drugs, he had the booze as insurance. The E he'd bounced from a dealer in Kennington Tube Station.

Letting back his head he howled: 'Had us a time, Meyer.'

Towards the close of the night's festivities, the sergeant, way down on the other side of the ecstasy moon, began to munch the doggie treats, intended as a surprise for Meyer, whispering: 'Bit salty, but not bad, no.'

Albert was miming before the mirror: 'I'm a believer…' and occasionally he'd give what he believed to be an impish grin like Davy Jones. Till a shadow fell across him.

Kevin.

'What the fuck are you doing? And turn off that shit.'

He aimed a kick at the hi-fi and the Monkees screeched to a halt. Albert rushed across to rescue the album. Sure enough, it was deeply scratched. He wailed: 'Whatcha want to do that for?'

Kevin gave a nasty laugh. 'Don't be so bleedin' wet. It can only improve those wankers, give 'em that unplugged feel. Now pay attention, I want to show you somefin'.'

He bent down and pulled out a long box from under the couch. He flipped the lid off and took out a rifle, said: 'Feast yer eyes on this, isn't it a beauty?'

'Is it real?'

'Real? You friggin' moron. It's a Winchester 460 Magnum. See that 'scope? Pick the hair outta yer nose from a rooftop.'

He pulled the bolt all the way back. A cartridge in the chamber slid home and he swung the barrel round into Albert's face, said: 'Grab some sky, pilgrim.'

'What?'

'Put yer bleedin' hands up.'

Albert slowly did so and Kev leaned closer, whispering: 'Make yer peace, Mister.'

'Kev!'

The gun went up an inch above Albert's head, then the trigger was pulled. The impact slammed the stock into his shoulder and knocked him back. The bullet tore into the wall, decanting a plastic duck. Albert stood in open-mouthed shock, and Kev, on his ass, on the floor, exclaimed: 'Fuck me, now that's fire power. What a rush.'

'Like a bad actor, memory always goes for effect.'

James Sallis, Black Hornet

Brant comes to and hears the most awful screeching, like someone is tearing the skin off a cat. Someone is indeed tearing the skin off a cat, on *The Simpsons*, in the 'Itchy and Scratchy' cartoon. The noise is deafening and Brant reaches up to turn it off. Pain in the major league as his body moves. His arse naked and he shudders to think why. But thank fuck he didn't go out... did he? His mind was careering in every direction. From one side surfaced a recent documentary he'd seen on the American Marine Corps. No matter what shit went down, they'd up, kick ass and shout: 'Semper Fi!'

He gave a weak attempt at it now, but it came out like a piss – flat and narrow. Then he rolled onto his stomach and visualised a harsh five military push-ups, and tried.

'Semp—'

And collapsed, muttering: 'Bollocks.'

Brant finally got to his feet, limped to the shower, caught sight of himself in the mirror.

Bad idea.

Pot belly. No, worse, a drooping one. Grey hair on his chest like sad brillo pads. He thought of the word 'bedraggled', said: 'I'm bedraggled.'

Too kind. It just didn't cut it. Call it fucked, more like. The shower was all he knew of heaven and hell, then to the medicine cabinet and two, no, fuck it, three Alka Seltzer. Ahh. Oh shit oh sweet Mary and Joseph, stay down. Nope. Up comes a technicolour yawn. Sweat pouring down his body, he couldn't pull his head up and so saw the multicoloured spread. Yup, there's the Seltzer. Useless fuckers, and be-gods, is that an E? Gimmie an E... gimme an... oomph-ah Paul McGrath. Now he tried again, with Andrews Liver Salt, and popped two soluble aspirin in the milk. Here we go.

Oh yes, there is a God, it stayed. Took one more shower. He knew a sharp belt of booze would fix him right up for an hour or less, and from there, it's flake city.

True, he'd managed to get Sally back for a time. Had sworn all the promises. Would have done it on the bible if needed. But alas, he couldn't make the pledge in his heart, where it most counted. Through work, booze and the sulking silences, he'd lost her all over again.

Then, as the caffeine danced along his nerve endings, he vaguely remembered young Tone. Oh shit, the kid had come to the door. Brant lit a shaky Weight, and tried to change mental tack. He couldn't recall what he'd said to the lad, but oh, oh he knew it was rough. Was it ever otherwise?

He turned to shout for Meyer Meyer, then remembered that too.

Atonement in white

'I like Jamiroquai,' said Tone.
'Yeah? Me, I like Tricky.'
'Yeah.'
He knew if he said yeah a bit, it gave him cool. Not ice or brain-dead, but hip without pushing it. Like he had attitude without having to work at it. He badly wished he'd brought his Bans, just let those shades sit easy on his face. As it was, the smoke was killing his eyes. He'd decided to get a lead on the band-aid duo, prove to Brant that HE was the bollocks. To his surprise, he'd gained entrance to the club on Railton without any hassle. True, they'd charged him 'instant membership', a straight twenty-five and then admission. But hey, he was in – this was the place – the happening, he was Serpico, undercover, he was cookin'.

Clubs in Brixton change overnight. What's hot on Tuesday is vacant city on Thursday. So it goes, they let Tone in 'cos he had cash, he was yer punter, yer John, yer actual Jimmy Wanker.

Shortly after he sat down, the girl put chat on him. Then he casually mentioned the band-aid people and she asked: 'Whatcha want them for?'

'Oh, nothing bad. In fact, I've a few quid owing them.'

She gave a mischievous laugh, said: 'Give it here. I'll see they get it.'

He laughed too. One of those clued-in jobs. Like he could dig it, yeah, go with the flow. She said: 'See the new weapon of choice?'

'What?'

'Yer baseball bat, it's passé. It's clubs now, like golf clubs.'

'Yeah?'

'Sure, since the black kid won that big golf thing.'

'The Masters.'

'What?'

'Nothing. Go on. '

'Yeah, well, that's what they're bouncing off skulls now.'

'Tee-off.'

'What?'

He ordered two more drinks and felt he was really blending. She said: 'Back in a sec.'

Which she wasn't. More like an hour. During which a huge black guy took her seat and her drink, eye-balling Tone all the while. Finally he asked: 'Now who I be?'

'Ahm.'

'I be the Archangel Tuafer.'

Tone tried to think of what Brant would say, something like: 'Hot enough for yer?' like that. What he said was: 'Uh. Uh.'

Then the girl appeared, slapped the guy on the back, said: 'Move on, big ass.'

He did. Tone said: 'He thinks he's an Archangel.'

'He's a divil all right.'

He tried to place her accent. I sounded like Dublin, but only sometimes. Then she said: 'C'mon, I can show you where those people are squatting.'

When they found Tone's body, he was naked, he'd been stabbed repeatedly and his head was bashed in. Roberts said: 'Jeez, if I had to guess, I'd say someone put a golf club to him.'

Brant was too ill to be outright sick, but he sure wanted to be. He said nothing.

Roberts continued: 'I saw him you know, that evening.'

'Yeah?'

'He was thinking of going to see you.'

'Was he?'

'Yeah. So did he?'

'Did he what, Guv?'

'Jeez, wake up man. Come to see you!'

'I dunno.'

'What?'

'I was out of it.'

'Christ, keep that to yourself.'

'Okay.'

Roberts knelt down, stared at the battered face, said: 'He'd a pair of Farahs, you know.'

'What?'

'Those smart pants, Jeez, I hope they didn't do him for a bloody pair of trousers.'

'Round here, Guv, they'd do you for a hankie.'

'Too bloody right.'

Brant thought, what a slogan for a company: *Would you kill for a pair of Farahs?*

But said nowt, he didn't think Roberts would appreciate it. He did half want to tell him about the wreath. How, when he opened his door that morning, there it was. A poor excuse of a wreath, but plainly recognisable. The flowers were withered, wilted and wan. In fact it seemed as if someone had first trampled on them. Even the ribbon was dirty. And get this, someone had bitten it.

Was it for him or Meyer, or both, or fuck? No big leap of detection to deduce, it was from The Umpire. Roberts would ask, if he'd been told: 'How do you know it was him? Mebbe kids took it from the cemetery, decided to wind you up.'

Then Brant would pause, look crestfallen, humbly take his hand from behind his back, and dah-dah! A cricket ball. Say: ''Cos this was nestling smack in the centre. Deduce that, ya prick.'

> 'That is not dead which
> can eternal lie. And with
> strange aeons even death
> may die.'

HP Lovecraft, The Necronomicon

How the Umpire giggled as he laid the wreath at Brant's door. He'd had to bite down on his hand to stop, lest he be heard.

The Euro-hit from a few years back, 'Hey Magdalene', was jammed in his head and he hummed with forced repetition. Had he known the wild abandon the ordained had danced with in hordes on Ibiza to this song, he might have taken pause.

Deliriously oblivious to past trends, he hummed as if he meant it. He couldn't believe the rush it was to tease, torment and outright taunt the police. When the cricket mob were done, he'd have to have a serious look at the Met. So much work, so little time.

He hummed on. Shannon felt so wired, he couldn't stop walking. He saw sparks light up his steps and found himself in the middle of Westminster Bridge. On impulse, he threw the Marks & Spencer bag over. It contained the crossbow.

Then he decided to suddenly cross the road. Without pause, he walked out into the traffic and a 159 bus lifted him about six feet and he fell back onto the pavement. As if the bus had said: 'Get back there, asshole.'

Passers-by gathered round, and a buzz of observations danced above him.

'Did you see that?'

'Walked right out in front of it.'

'Pissed as a parrot.'

'What a wanker.'

An ambulance was eventually called, but it got caught in the rush. Its siren wailed uselessly, but loud enough to irritate the shit out of the stalled motorists.

And speaking of wreaths

They buried Jacko Mary on a cold November morning long after *A White Arrest* was concluded. There was the grave-digger, Roberts and a shabby woman. When the coffin was down, she said: 'Rough enough to die alone.'

'You're here.'

'I'm not a friend. He owed me money.'

Roberts tried to temper his anger. 'Thought you might still get it, eh?'

''Ere, don't be sarky. You must be that copper.'

Roberts looked round, said: 'Yeah. Keep it down, OK?'

'He liked you, he did.'

'Really?'

'Oh yeah. Were he any good as a snitch, like?'

Roberts considered. Jacko Mary had cracked the 'E' case, sort of, but he said: 'No.'

'Didn't fink so.'

As a cop, Roberts had to do lots of dodgy things, came with the territory. But this denial was to be one act he felt forever ashamed about.

At a squat in Coldharbour Lane, a woman was stirring. 'Tony.'

She raised her voice. 'Tony!'

'What? What's going on?'

'Brew us a cup o' tea, two sugars.'

'Fock off.'

She got up and gave him a smack on the head with an old copy of the *Big Issue*. If she'd checked, Tricky was on the cover. He got up and moved over to the gas ring. Near tripped on a number nine club. The grip was worn, well used. The woman watched him as he tried to get it together to light the gas, said:

'Jaysus, yer arse looks great in them Farahs.'

'They're a bit tight, cut into the crack of my hole.'

And he moved his right leg to demonstrate. She said: 'Naw, I like 'em.'

'D'ya think I'm sexy?'

'Yeah, dead sexy.'

In Coldharbour Lane, Kevin had called a meet. He was dressed in combat gear, and wired to the moon. Doug and Fenton exchanged wary glances. Albert arrived late and got a bollocking.

'What is it, Albert, yer getting tired of our crusade, that it?'

'I had to sign on, Kev. I was up the DHSS.'

'Yer head is up yer ass, is what. Time to get yer attention, fella. Time to get everybody's attention.'

He threw three black-and-white photos on the coffee table, said: 'We're moving up.'

Albert felt his heart thump, tried: 'Like another area?'

Kevin crossed to him, began to jab his chest with his fingers, jabbed hard, spitting: 'No shithead, we're staying put, no scum's running me outta my manor. We're gonna off three fucks at once.'

Fenton was on his feet: 'What? C'mon Kevin, how the hell are we gonna pull that off?'

Kevin didn't look at him, but continued to jab at his brother, said: 'See these three, yeah in the photies, they've set up shop together. Got a co-op in Electric Avenue and that's where we're gonna take 'em.'

Doug sighed, asked:

'And the three guys, they're just gonna say, "Hey OK, we'll come with youse – oh, nice rope."'

Kevin's eyes gleamed, his moment, said: 'That's it Douggie, we'll do them in their gaff.'

A week later…

At the CA Club, Cora was gushing energetically.
'But Penelope, are you sure you won't let one of the boys pamper you?

'No! Is there something you can't grasp? Try this: N-O!'

'Oh golly, we seem a trifle tense today. Perhaps a drinkipoos?'

'Ah, for heaven's sake!' And she snapped to her feet, began to pace. Cora fussed on: 'Your friend seemed keenish, I do believe she has a minor crush on our Jason.'

Penny glared at her, said: 'Get bloody real!'

The door chimes went. Today they played 'Uno Paloma Blanca', it added to Penny's bile. Cora said: 'Excuse me lambikins, but I must see to that. Don't you just die with those chimes?'

Cora lightly patted her frosted hair before answering the door. The hair was rigid and today resembled an off-kilter meringue mess. She opened the door.

Brant said: 'Yo, Cora, how they hanging?'

A fraction later, she tried to slam it. He gave it a push, knocking her back inside. Falls followed behind, like the biblical pale rider. Cora tried for indignation: 'How dare you? I trust you have a warrant?'

Brant stepped right up to her, said, 'It's bloody Maggie Johnson… I wondered where you'd legged it to. My, my, come up in the world, 'aven't you? Here, constable, this is Maggie, the cheapest ride this side of the Elephant 'n' Castle.'

Cora raised her voice. 'Damn impertinence, you've overstepped your brief, sonny. We're protected.'

Brant drew an almighty kick to Cora's knee and she dropped like a stone. He hunkered down, tried unsuccessfully to grasp her hair, and settled for her neck, said, 'What the fuck kind of shit you got in yer hair? Now listen up, don't back-talk me, ever, or I'll break yer nose… OK?'

She nodded. He caught her shoulder and hoisted her up, said: 'Let's hobble inside, see what's cookin'.'

On seeing Penny, Falls nearly spoke, but settled for a look; one of pure malice. Brant pushed Cora into a chair, asked Penny:

'Room number?'

'It's not numbers, it's names.'

'So gimme the bloody name.'

'The Cherise Room, upstairs, first on the right.'

'OK, now hop it.'

'I can go?'

'Yeah, fuck off.'

Cora wanted to shout abuse, to tear at Penny's eyes, but Brant said: 'Don't ever think about it.'

When the door had closed, Brant turned to Falls, said, 'Keep yer eyes on this cow. If she even twitches, give her a clout round the ear-hole.'

Fiona was over an orgasmic rainbow. Jason, between her legs working like a bastard. Moans and cries punctuated the seizures of her body. The door crashed open and Brant said:

'Tasty.'

Jason turned his head, confusion, shock, writ large. His brain whispered 'husband'.

Fiona tried to sit up, pushed against Jason and grabbed for a sheet. Brant closed the door and leant against it, began to light a Weight as the pair fumbled on the bed.

He said, 'Hey, don't stop on my account.'

Eventually, Jason got his briefs on, and Fiona pulled the sheet up to her chin.

Brant smiled, then reached back to open the door. 'Off yah go, cocker.'

As Jason edged past to get out, Brant gave him a hefty

slap on the arse and shut the door behind him. He turned to Fiona. 'Get dressed then.'

Fiona was trying to calm her roaring mind, said: 'How can I, with you standing there?'

He gave a hearty laugh. 'Jaysus, I've seen what you've got. Now move it or I'll dress you.'

She did. Shame and bewilderment crowded down as she pulled her clothes on. Brant's eyes never left her.

Then she said, 'I'm ready.'

'Whoo-kay, I'll drive you home.'

'What?'

'You don't wanna walk, Fiona. Not after the exertion you've been putting in. Naw, the motor's outside.'

Fiona gave a last shot at comprehension. 'You're not taking me to my husband?'

'What? naw, whatcha think I am, some kind of animal?' Brant put Fiona in the front of a battered Volkswagen Golf, said to Falls:

'You'll be all right from here, there's a tube down the road.'

Falls didn't like any of this, said: 'Shouldn't I be along as a witness?' He gave a snide chuckle, a dangerous sound. 'Wise up, babe.'

She put her hand on the door, insisting. 'I'm sorry, Sarge, but I feel I should…'

He pushed her hand away, losing it a little.

'Piss off, Falls, you're drawing attention. Don't ever do that to me.'

She backed off. He moved in close, anger leaking through his eyes. 'You want to worry about something, Falls? Worry about paying me back.'

He slammed the door, causing Falls to shudder. Then he moved to the driver's side, got in and slammed the door, burnt rubber leaving. Falls watched them go and gritted her teeth.

'OK, I'll pay you back you bastard, and BIG TIME.'

Brant looked at Fiona and winked.

She asked: 'Where are you taking me?'

'Hey, relax, go along for the ride.' A pause. 'Whoops, sorry! As they say, you've been there, done that, and did you ever. That Jason, eh? For a half-wog, he was hung.'

If there was a reply, she didn't have it, and tried to crawl way within herself. There wasn't a place that far away. Brant pulled up on the Walworth Road, parked carelessly on a double yellow.

'I thought Carter Street nick had closed?'

'Tut-tut, restless girls get spanked. C'mon, get out.'

He escorted her to a transport caff near Marks & Spencers, pushed her inside, found a back table. The table was alight with dead chips, rasher rinds and toast crumbs. Brant seemed delighted, said: 'If it's not on the table, it's not on the menu.'

'It's disgusting.'

'You'd know.'

A waitress in her fifties came over. She'd obviously had disappointing news in her teens and wasn't yet recovered. Her face seemed unfinished without a tired cigarette. She said:

'Yeah?'

Brant knew the risk of towing Fiona round his own manor but it gave a kick.

He said: 'Two sausages, egg, bacon, puddin', and two rounds of buttered toast.'

He looked at Fiona.

'You've got to be kiddin'.'

Brant smiled at the waitress, said, 'She'll have the same, and throw in a family pot of tea.' As the waitress turned to go, he added, 'The smile needs some work, OK?'

The waitress ignored him.

Fiona stared at him and asked, 'You don't seriously think I'll eat that garbage?'

'Oh you will, *and* like it.'

He didn't move, but she felt the physical presence of him. It rolled across the table to taunt and threaten her.

119

He touched the once-white tablecloth.

'Gingham would have worked.'

'Excuse me?'

'For the table; you know, a woman's touch. I like the touch of a woman.' He took out the Weights. 'Do you?'

She shook her head and knew the 'no smoking' edict hadn't penetrated here. The food came, and after the plates were set down, Brant asked, 'Where's that smile?'

But his attention was diverted as two people entered the caff. He recognised the Band Aids, and they clocked him. Turned right about and legged it. He thought, 'Later,' and pared a wedge of sausage, nodded to Fiona.

'Eat.'

She tried.

He poured scalding tea into mugs, raised his, said: 'Get that down yah, girl.'

She tasted it and nearly threw up. It was greasy, seemingly heavily sugared and tasted of tobacco. She put the mug down, said: 'OK, you've had your fun.'

'What? I'm having me grub, but no, I've not had me fun. Not yet.'

'What is it you want, exactly?'

He took out a surprisingly clean handkerchief, dabbed delicately at the corners of his mouth, said:

'I'd like to be your suitor.'

Maybe my future starts right now.

John Garfield: Voice-over, The Postman Always Rings Twice.

As Falls prepared her shopping list, she fantasised being a Goth. Just for one outing. She couldn't stand The Cure and, if that was music… yeah. But the gear, all those black dresses and the death white make-up. Ah, dream on…

They'd love it down the nick. She could just hear Brant's war cry: 'I could ride that.'

The man would get up on a cat. She was dressed for shopping. Reeboks (off white) Tracksuit (one white)

And a large carrier bag. Black. Daren't be seen to 'Accessorise', very ungothic. She'd been reading an article headlined 'SO, WHAT KIND OF SHOPPER ARE YOU?'

Retail analysts divide shoppers into six types, they use this information to attract the shoppers they want, and deter others. Supermarkets will tempt the Comfortable and Contented with displays of minor luxuries. Mainstream Mercenaries will be deterred by supermarkets offering either lack of choice, or too much.

Falls was a sucker for quizzes. Forever completing *News of the World* magazine questions like 'What kind of lover are you?'

She read aloud the first three types of shopper:

1. Mainstream Merchant: The retailer's least favourite group – low budget shoppers who buy only the cheapest goods on sale. Impervious to the siren-call of exotic foods.

2. *Struggling Idealist:* scrutinise every label for contents, buy only eco-sensitive soap powder. Ozone friendliness very important.

3. *Self Indulgent:* self-explanatory. Very welcome in super-markets.

'Mmmm,' she thought. 'Alas, that first rings a bell. Then, the final three:

4. *Comfortable and Contented:* favourite with the retailer because these happy bunnies like to reward themselves with that extra tin of tuna ('Well, we do use a lot of it, and it is very healthy.') Delia Smith is their icon.

5. *Frenzied Coper:* fastest shopper in the west. Knows what she wants and where to get it, homes in on target sections at speed. Will not even spot the most seductive gondola or special-offer basket.

6. *Habit-Bound Die-Hard:* frugal but loyal; the mostly male section. Meat and two veg man, spuds and sprouts only, never mange tout. Buys six days' worth of food for £20. This (surprise, surprise) is the type the analysts have also dubbed the 'Victor Meldrew'

As she scanned No. 6, she thought, 'Oh God, I'll end up married to one of those.'

Crumpling the article, she threw it in the bin. On a T-shirt she'd seen once, the logo was: 'When the going gets tough, the tough go shopping.'

It seemed about right.

She strapped on her Walkman and was ready to roll, Sheryl Crow blasting loud.

At the entrance to the supermarket, she bought the *Big Issue* and the vendor said:

'Have a good one.'

She'd tried.

A gaggle of girls brushed past her, nearly knocking her over. One of them petulantly crying: 'Oh… ex-cuse me!' in *that* tone. What John L Williams describes as an 'Angela', a particular drawl that upper-class junkies seem to have patented: One part frightfully, frightfully; two parts frightfully fucked up. The type who insist on slimline tonic as they swill buckets of gin.

Falls got a trolley and turned off her Walkman. The supermarket had a loop tape, the same song 100 times. Today it was U2 with 'You're So Cruel.'

Killer tune, but over and over.

Reach for them razor blades or mainline Valium.

Falls knew the very next track should be 'The Fly'

Sounds like Bauhaus on speed. But course, due to the bloody loop, it never gets there.

She headed for the frozen veg.

If he was a colour, he'd be beige.

Past toiletries and disinfectants to see a kicking. A man was on the ground and three teenagers were putting the boot in. And kicking like they meant it. Steel caps on the toes flashed like treacherous zips of empty hope.

'Oi!' she roared.

Reaching for a tin (it was marrowfats) she lobbed it high and fast. It bounced off the first kid like whiplash. He dropped like a sack of thin flower, and the others legged it.

People were shouting and coming up behind her. She got to the man on the ground and saw he was in uniform. Security. Blood was pouring down his face. He said: 'I showed them, eh?' She smiled and helped him up. His brown hair was falling into his eyes and she clocked startling blue eyes, big as neon. She felt her heart lurch and reprimanded herself mentally: 'Don't be daft, it couldn't be.'

She said: 'We'd better get you seen to.'

'Like a cat is it?'

As he stood up she saw he was just the right height, a hazy six foot, and that they'd look good together. A man came striding up, all shit, piss and wind: the manager. He barked: 'What on earth is going on?' and glanced at the teenager who was stirring and moaning. Falls said: 'The apprentice thug there was apprehended by your security, at great physical cost.'

The manager barked louder: 'But he's just a boy, what's wrong with him?'

'He got canned.'

Falls accompanied the security guard for aid. To the pub. He ordered a double brandy and she a Britvic orange, slim-line. She put out her hand, said: 'I'm glad to meet you. And you are?'

'Beige. That's how I feel, but put me on the other side of that drink, I'll be, as Stephanie Nicks sang, "A Priest of Nothingness".'

His Irish brogue surfaced haphazardly as he lilted on some of the words, then he added: 'I'm Eddie Dillon.'

'Dylan?'

'Naw, the other one, the Irish fella.'

'He's famous?'

'Not yet, but he's game.'

She laughed, said: 'I haven't one clue to what you're on about.'

He gave a shy smile, answered: 'Ah, there's no sense in it, but it has a grand ring!' He looked at her hands, added: 'And speaking of rings, can I hope yer not wed?'

She was filled with warmth, not to mention a hint of lust. She said: 'Are you long in security?'

He drained his glass and she clocked his even white teeth. He said: 'I was with the Social Security for longer than either of us admit, but yes, it's what I do. I like minding things. I used to do it back home, but that's a long time ago. Thank Jaysus… and no, it's not what I do while I'm waiting to be an actor. I'm with Woody Allen who said he was an actor till he got an opening as a waiter.'

She laughed again, then said: 'I've got shopping to do, so are you going to ask me out?'

'I might.'

Roberts looked at his wife across the breakfast table. Deep lines were etched around her eyes, and he thought: 'Good Lord, she's aging.' But said: 'England went under with barely a whimper, losing their final match by twenty-eight runs today.'

'That's hardly surprising dear, surely?'

'Oh?'

'Well, I mean the poor lambs have a maniac stalking them. It's not conducive to good cricket, is it?'

He felt his voice rising: 'All they had to chase was a perfectly manageable victory target of 229.'

'Says you. And darling, I'm sure they feel you should be chasing a maniac instead of criticising.'

Falls was surprised that Eddie Dillon had a car. She felt he'd have a lot of surprises. The motor was a beat-up Datsun, faded maroon. He said:

'I won it off a guy in a card game.'

'What?'

'Just kidding. It's the kind of line guys adore to use.'

'Why?'

'Good question, and one I have no answer to.'

He was dressed in a thin suit; everything about it was skinny, from the labels to the crease. A startling white shirt cried: 'Clean, oh yes.' Falls had her sedate hooker ensemble. Black low-cut dress, short, and black tights. Slingback heels that almost promised comfort, but not quite. He said: 'You look gorgeous.'

She knew she looked good. In fact, before he arrived, she'd almost turned herself on. He'd brought a box of Dairy Milk. The big motherfucker that'd feed a flock of nuns.

She asked: 'Won them in a card game?'

'Yup, two aces over five, does it every third hand.'

'Where are we going?'

'To Ireland.'

And in a sense, they did.

'I was a small time crook until this very minute, and now I'm a big-time crook!'

Clifton Young in Dark Passage

Fenton, of the 'E' gang, was becoming less wallpaperish. He was beginning, for the first time in his life, to follow the plot. Not completely, but definitely in there. Now, coming off a football high, he challenged Kevin, said: 'See that young copper got done?'

'Yeah.'

'The papers are saying we done it.'

Kev was dressed in urban guerrilla gear. Tan combat pants with all the pockets, tan singlet and those dogtags they sell in the arcade. Desert Storm via Brixton. He sensed Fen's attitude and squared off. A Browning automatic peaking from the pocket on his left thigh. He smiled, said: 'Fuck 'em.'

Fenton, less sure, wanted to back off, but had to hold. Asked: 'Did ya, Kev? Did ya do him?'

Kev was well pleased. It kept the troops in line if they believed the boss was totally not to be fucked with. He said: 'Whatcha fink Fen, eh… what do ya reckon, matey?' Now Albert and Doug were on their feet and the air was crackling. Fen fell back into a chair, saying: 'Aw Jeez, Kev, you never said nuffing about doing the old bill. Jeez, it's not on. It's not…' And he groped in desperation for a word to convey his feeling. 'It's not British.'

Kev gave a wild laugh, then pulled the Browning out, got into shooter stance, legs apart, two-handed grip, swung the barrel back and forth across his gang, shouted: 'Incoming!'and watched the fucks dive for cover.

He could hear hueys fly low over the Mekong Delta, and vowed to re-rent *Apocalypse Now*.

'What a place. I can feel the rats in the wall.'

Phantom Lady

The Galtimore Ballroom confirms the English nightmare. That the Irish are: One, tribal. Two, ferocious. Three, stone mad.

To see a heaving mass of hibernians 'dancing' to a showband with an abandon of insecurity, is truly awesome. Like a rave with intent. When Falls saw the entrance and felt the vibes, she asked: 'Are we here to dance or to raid?'

Eddie took her hand, laughed: 'They're only warming up.'

She could only hope this was a joke.

It wasn't. Two bouncers at the door said in unison: 'How ya, Eddie.'

Falls didn't know: was this good or bad? Good that he was known, but how regular was he? Was she just another in a line of Saturday Night Specials, cheap and over the counter?

Eddie said: 'They're Connemara men. Never mess with them. When penance is required, they think true suffering is to drink sherry.'

Inside it was sweltering, and seemed like all of humanity had converged. Eddie said: 'Wait here, I'll get some minerals,' and was gone.

Falls panicked, felt she'd never see him again. The sheer mass of the crowd moved her along and into the ballroom. She thought: 'So this is hell.'

A stout man, reeking of stout in a sweat stained shirt asked her: 'D'yer want a turn?'

'No thank you, I'm—' but he shouted: 'Stick it, yer black bitch!'

A band, consisting of at least fifty or so it seemed, were doing a loud version of 'I Shot the Sheriff'. Mainly it was loud, and they sure hated the sheriff. And here was Eddie, big smile, two large iced drinks, saying: 'So, did you miss me?'

'Yeah.'

Then they were dancing, despite the crowd, the heat and the band. They were cookin'. He could jive like an eel. Falls had never met a man who could dance. In fact most of them could barely speak. It deeply delighted her. Then a slow number: 'Miss You Nights'.

And she drew him close, enfolded him tight. She asked: 'Is that a poem or are you real pleased with me?'

'It's poetry all right.'

And later, it would be.

The Beauty of Balham

Falls was in love with love. She yearned to feel the mix of sickness, nausea and exhilaration that came with it. So in love you couldn't eat, sleep or function. The telephone ruled your life and ruined it. Would he phone, and when, if, oh God…

You bastard. She wanted to do crazy shit like write their married name and buy him shirts he'd never wear. Cut his hair and hang out with his family, prattle on about him until her friends roared: 'Enough!'

Lie awake all night and stare at his face, trace his lips gently with two fingers and half hope he'd wake. Kiss him before he shaved and wear the beard rash like a trophy. Mess his hair just after he'd carefully styled it, and iron his laundry, or even iron his face. She giggled. Publicly, on matters musical, she'd drop the name of cool like Alanis Morissette. Sing the lyrics of mild obscenity and mouth the words of kick ass. At home, if it wasn't the Cowboy Junkies, she'd tie her hair in a severe bun and put Evita on the turntable. Her window had a flower box, and with the tiniest push of imagination – open that window full – she was on the balcony of the Casa Rosada in Buenos Aires. A couple of dry sherries fuelled the process and she'd sing along with 'Don't Cry for me, Argentina'.

The track on total repeat till tears formed in her eyes, her heart near burnt from tenderness for her 'shirtless ones'. Till a passer-by shouted: 'Put a bloody sock in it!'

It's not beyond the bounds of possibility that, at odd times, her voice carried to the Umpire, and eased the dreams of carnage he'd envisaged. Reluctantly, like a sad Peronist, she shut Evita down and considered her situation. If she told Roberts about Brant and Mrs Roberts, she was in deep shit. If she didn't tell him and he found out, she was in deeper mire. If she said nowt to nobody, she'd probably survive. It stuck in her gut like the benign cowardice it was. Falls could vividly remember the day her friends ran up to her in the street saying: 'Come quick, look at the man on the common.'

When she got there, her heart sank. The object of their curiosity was her dad. Staggering home from the pub after a day's drinking. She tried to help him. She was four years old. As long as she could remember, her life had been overshadowed by his drinking. He was never violent, but it cast a huge cloud over the family. She felt she was born onto a battlefield. His booze destroyed the family. With it came with the four horsemen: Poverty, Fear, Frustration, Despair.

Dad was anaesthetised from all that. There was never money for schoolbooks or food. Nights were spent trying to block out her parents' raised voices. Or curled up, too terrified to sleep because her father hadn't come home. Wishing he was dead and praying he wasn't. Never inviting her friends home as her father's moods were unpredictable. Most of her childhood spent covering up for his drinking. Once, asking him: 'Can I have two shillings for an English book?'

'Sure, don't you speak it already?'

Whispering, lest his sleep be disturbed. All of this destroyed her mother. Being of Jamaican descent, she developed the 'tyrant syndrome', and tried to enlist young Falls on her side. Early she learned to 'run with the hare and savage with the hound'. Oh yes! Then she became convinced that mass would help. If she went to church enough, he'd stop.

He didn't.

She stopped church. Slowly, she realised the terrible dilemma for such a child as she. They have to recover from the alcoholic parent they had, and suffer for the one they

132

didn't have. When she was nineteen she had a choice: go mad or get a career. Thus she'd joined the police and often felt it was indeed a mobile madness.

'Love makes the world
go round'

Falls, looking in the mirror, said: 'I am gorgeous.' She sure felt it. Eddie told her all the time, and wow, she never got tired of it. For no reason at all, he'd touched her cheek, saying: 'I can't believe I found you.' Jesus!

A woman dreams her whole life of such a man. If all his lines were just lines, so what? It was magic. She was sprinkled in stardust. True, she'd tried the clichés, the mush on toast of trying out his name to see how it fit: 'Susan Dillon.'

Mmm. How about Susan Falls Dillon?

Needed work.

Eddie Dillon rolled off Falls, lay on his back and exhaled. 'The Irishman's Dream.'

'What's that, then?'

'To fuck a policeman.'

After the dance, she'd asked him for a drink. He'd had her. In the hall, the kitchen, the sitting room and finally, panting, he'd said: 'I give up – where have you hidden the bed?'

As they lay on the floor, knackered, the age-old divide between the sexes was full frontal. She wanted him to hold her and tell her he loved her, to luxuriate in the afterglow. He wanted to sleep. But new-mannish educated as he partly was, he compromised. Held her hand and dozed. She had to bite her tongue not to say 'I love you.' Then he stirred, said: 'I've a thirst on me to tempt the Pope. I'll give you a fiver to spit in me mouth.'

She laughed and, victim of the new emancipation, rose and got him a pint of water. After he'd drunk deep, he gave a huge burp, rested the glass on his chest, said: 'Jaysus, a man could love a woman like you.'

Ah! The perennial bait, the never-fail, tantalising lure of the big one. Her heart pounding, she knew she was in the relationship minefield. One foot wrong and boom, back to Tesco's pre-frozen for one. She said: 'I hope you were careful.' He tilted the glass slightly, said: 'Oh yes, I didn't spill a drop.'

When finally they went to bed, he slept immediately. Falls hated how much she wanted to be held. Later, she was woken by him thrashing and screaming, and then he sat bolt upright. She said: 'Oh God, are you OK?'

'Man, the flashbacks.'

'What?'

'Isn't that what the guys always say in the movies?'

'Oh.'

'Jesus, it was some movie.'

As Falls settled back to uneasy sleep, she ran Tony Braxton's song in her head – 'Unbreak My Heart'.

Eddie had all the moves. After he'd spent a night at her flat, next day she'd discover little notes, tucked in the fridge, under the pillow, the pocket of her coat. All of the ilk: 'I miss you already', or 'You are the light in my darkness', And other gems. Mills and Boon would have battled for him. Walking together, he'd say: 'Can I take yer hand, it makes me feel total warmth.'

A God.

And what a kisser. Finally, a man born to lip service. She could have come with kissing alone and did often.

> 'If your dead father comes
> to you in a dream, he
> comes with bad news. If
> your dead mother comes,
> she brings good news.'

Rosie couldn't decide which coffee. She and Falls had met at one of the new specialty coffee cafés. The menu contained over thirty types of brew. Falls said: 'Good Lord, I suppose instant is out of the question.'

'Shh, don't think such heresy, the windows will crack in protest.'

Falls took another pan of the list, then said: 'OK, I'll have the double latté.'

'What?'

'I know the names from the movies.'

'Mmm, sounds weak. I'll have the Seattle Slam.' They laughed.

Rosie said: 'So, girl. Tell all, can you?'

Falls giggled, said: 'If I tell you he kisses the neck…'

'Uh-huh.'

'…right below the hairline.'

'Oh God, a prince.'

'And holds you after.'

'He is unique, beyond prince.'

The coffee came and Falls sampled it, said: 'Yeah, it's instant with froth.' Then she leaned closer, added: 'You know why I did, like, on the first date?'

136

''Cos you're a wanton cow.'

'That too. But when we came out of the dance, I felt faint.'

'Lust, girl.'

'And I sat on the pavement.'

Rosie made a face as she tasted her drink, telling Falls to continue.

'Before I could, he whipped off his jacket and laid it on the path.'

'So you sat on it and later you sat on his face.'

They roared, shamefully delighted, warmly scandalised. Rosie said: 'Taste this,' and pushed the slam across. Falls did, said: 'It's got booze in there, check the menu.'

Sure enough, in the small print, near illegible, was: 'Pure Colombian beans, double hit of espresso, hint of Cointreau.' Falls said: 'I know what the Cointreau's hinting.'

'What's that, then?'

'Get bladdered. Did I tell you I dreamed of my dad?'

Later, wired on slammers, hopping on espresso, Falls showed her Eddie Dillon's poem.

'He wrote a poem for you?'

'Yes.' (shyly)

'Is it any good?'

'Who cares? 'Cos it's for me, it's brilliant.'

'Give it here, girl!'

She did.

Benediction

Never believed
in such as blessings
were
you threw
a make
un-helped, upon the day
and help available
was how you helped
yourself – A crying
down
to but a look in caution – stayed alert
reducing always towards
the basic front
in pain
– never
– never the once
to once admit
you floundering had to be

Such Gods as crossed
your mind – if God
as such it
might have been
you never took
to vital introspection

Such it was from you
did feel
the very first in love's belief
form feaming every smile
you ever freely
gave

Rosie's lips moved as she read. For some reason, this touched Falls and she had to look away. Finally: 'Wow, it's deep.'

''Tis. that's what he says, "'tis".'

'Do you understand it?'

'Course not. What's that got to do with anything?'

'Oh, you lucky cow, I think I hate you!'

Virgin? What's your problem. Whore? What's your number.

Naomi Wolf (Rocking Years)

Sent flowers every other day, she said: 'I am blessed full. Not a cloud to be seen... almost. One or two tiny niggles, hardly worth consideration: one, he couldn't take her to his flat; two, she couldn't phone him. Weighted against the other gold, these were nothing – right?

Rightish! No point even sharing those with Rosie. Why bother? But: 'Rosie, whatcha think about..?' And Rosie: 'Oh God, that's very ominous.'

Falls was raging: 'Ominous? When did you swallow a dictionary?' That's it, no more input from Ms Know-it-all.

The doorbell went and she felt her heart fly. At a guess, more roses. With a grin, she opened the door.

Not Interflora.

A bag lady. Well, next best thing. A middle-aged woman who could be kindest described as 'frumpy', and you'd be reaching. Her hair was dirt grey, and whatever shade it had been, that was long ago. Falls sighed. The homeless situation was even worse than the *Big Issue*'s warnings. Now they were making house calls. She geared herself for action: arm lock, a few pounds and the address of the Sally... she'd be history.

The woman said: 'Are you WPC Falls, the policewoman?'

Surprisingly soft voice. The new Irish cultured one of soft vowels and easy lilt, riddled with education.

'Yes.'

'I'm Nora.'

Falls tried not to be testy, said: 'I don't wish to be rude, but you say it as if it should mean something. It doesn't mean anything to me.'

The woman stepped forward, not menacingly, but more as if she didn't want the world to hear, said: 'Nora Dillon, Eddie's wife.'

Falls had dressed for confrontation. The requisite Reeboks, sweatshirt and pants. She sat primly on her couch, letting Eddie hang himself. First, she'd considered sitting like Ellen Degenes. That sitcom laid-back deal, legs tucked under your butt, yoga-esque. Mainly cool, like très. But it hurt like a son-of-a-bitch. Since Dyke City, when Ellen had come out of the closet, was she a role model? 'We think not,' said Middle America. So, Eddie arrived with red roses, Black Magic and a shit-eating grin. He's even quoting some of his poetry. Like this:

I gave you then
a cold hello
and you
being poorer
gave me nothing
nothing at all.

He was dressed in a tan linen suit with a pair of Bally loafers. His face looked carbolic-shined. He looked like a boy. It tore at her heart. Jesus. Now he was repeating the line for effect: 'Gave me nothing'. Lingering, slow-lidded look, then: '...nothing at all'.

Eddie looked up, awaiting praise. Falls got to her feet, said, 'Come here.'

He smiled, answered, 'I love it when you're dominant.'

He moved right to her, turned his head to kiss her and she kneed him in the balls, said, 'Rhyme that, you bastard.'

Dropped to the floor like a bad review. She thought of Brant and what he'd say.

'Finish it off with a kick to the head.'

Part of her was sorely tempted, but the other half wanted to hug him. Summoning all her resolve, she bent down and grabbed hold of the linen jacket and began to drag him. One of his tan loafers came off. Got him to the door and with the last of her strength, flung him out. Then she gathered up the flowers, the chocolates and the loose shoe, threw them after him. Then she slammed the door, stood with her back against it for a while, then slumped down to a sitting position.

After a time she could hear him. He tapped on the door and his voice,

'Honey… sweetheart… let me explain…'

Like a child, she put her fingers in her ears. It didn't fully work: she could still hear his voice but not the sense of the words. It continued for a time then gradually died away. Eventually she moved and got to her feet, said, 'I'm not going to cry anymore.'

She had a shower and had it scalding, till her skin screamed SURRENDER. Then she found a grubby track suit and climbed into it. It made her look fat.

She said, 'This makes me look fat… good!'

Opened the door cautiously. No Eddie. Some of the flowers still strewn around clutched at her heart.

Falls had seen all sorts of things in her police career, but these few flowers appeared to be the very essence of lost hope.

At the off-licence, she ordered a bottle of vodka and debated a mixer. But no, she'd take it bitter, it was fitting.

Back home, she drank the vodka from a mug. A logo on the side said: *I'm too sexy for my age.*

Bit later she put on Joan Armatrading and wallowed in total delicious torment.

Near the end of the bottle, she threw the music out of the window.

End of the evening, she took a hammer to the mug and bust it to smithereens.

Brant was booted and suited. The flat had been cleaned by a professional firm. They hadn't actually been paid yet, but assured of 'police protection'. He was well pleased with their work. The suit was genuine Jermyn Street bespoke. A burglary there had brought Brant to investigate... and pillage. If a look can speak columns, then this suit spoke like royalty. You could sleep in it and have it shout: 'Hey, is this class or what?'

It was. The shoes were hand-made Italian loafers and whispered of effortless arrogance. He wore a Police Federation tie, a blotch on any landscape, and a muted shirt. He gazed at himself in the new full-length mirror and was delighted, said: 'I ain't half delighted.' The whole outfit was clarion call to Muggers United till they saw his face, and rethought: 'Maybe not.'

He took his bleeper in case the 'E' rang. He needed access. A genuine Rolex completed the picture. Alas, it was so real it appeared a knock-off and supplied a badly needed irony to his whole appearance. He said aloud: 'Son, you are hot.' As he left he slammed his new steel-reinforced door with gusto.

It's been heard in south-east London that 'a copper's lot is a Volvo'. Brant was no exception. He found it a distinct advantage to have a recognisable cop issue. Saved it from being nicked. Others said: 'Who'd bloody want it?' As he unlocked his car, a few drops of rain fell. He said: 'Shit.' And remembered his old man one time, saying: 'Ah! Soft Irish rain.' His mother's reply: 'Soft Irish men, more like.'

A woman approached, dressed respectably, which revealed absolutely nothing. Not to Brant. She said: 'Excuse me?'

'What?'

'I hate to trouble you, but my car's broken down and I'm

without change. I need three, perhaps four pounds to get a cab.'

'You need a new line, lady.'

And he got into the Volvo. She watched him, astonishment writ large, and as he pulled away, she said clearly: 'Cunt.'

He laughed out loud. The night had begun well.

'Tooling up'

'Tonight... Tonight... Tonight... we go... oh yeah.'
On the floor, he'd spread a tarpaulin, and now began to lay weapons down: two sawn-offs, one canister of CS gas, three baseball bats and a mess of handguns.

He looked to his brother first, said: 'OK, Albert, pick yer poison.' Al took a handgun, tested it for weight, and then jammed it in the back of his jeans. Kev whistled: 'Very fucking cool. Mind how you sit down.'

He snatched the sawn-offs and chucked them to Doug and Fenton, said: ''Cos you guys are a blast.'

He took the handguns and, holding them down by his sides, added: 'No need for the bats, eh? This is purely a shooting party.' Albert smiled, thought of the gun he'd looted. Now he'd be truly loaded.

Fiona Roberts knew her marriage was bad, and often woesome. But she was determined to keep it. If it meant lying down with the dogs... or dog, then she'd suffer the fleas. She wasn't sure how to dress for a blackmail date. Did you go mainline hooker or bag lady? A blend of the two perhaps. When Brant had said he wished to 'woo' her, she'd nearly laughed in his pig face. But instinct had held her tongue and she knew she could maybe turn everything round. So she agreed, he was to pick her up at Marble Arch. Ruefully she reflected it was a hooker's landmark. A cab took her there and, as she paid the fare, the driver said: 'Bit cold for it, luv.'

'How dare you!'

'What?'

'Your implication. I don't think I know what you are saying.'

'Get a grip, darlin'. I didn't mean nuffink unless civility has been outlawed.'

'Hmmph!'

She slammed the door and he took off with her tenner.

Brant was turning into the Arch with the radio blaring. Chris Rea was doing 'Road to Hell' and Brant hoped it wasn't an omen. He stopped, flung open the door, shouted: 'Hiya, ducks!'

She'd been expecting the Volkswagen Golf, but realised he'd keep her on the hop. As she got in she saw him eying her legs but refrained from comment. Without a word he did a U-turn and swung back towards Bayswater. A highly dangerous move.

She said: 'Illegal, surely?'

'That's part of the rush.'

She smoothed her dress over her legs and he asked: 'Hungry?'

'Why, have you another greasy spoon to slum in?'

'Hey!' And he gave her a look. She could have sworn he appeared hurt and she thought: 'Good.'

He swerved to avoid a cyclist and said quietly: 'I've booked at Bonetti's.'

She didn't say anything, and he added: 'Well?'

'Well what? I have never heard of it.'

'It's in the Egon Ronnie.'

'Ronnie? That's Ronay.'

'Whatever, I thought you'd be pleased.'

And she was, kind of.

Roberts got the call before six. 'Chief Inspector Roberts, is that you?'

'Yeah.'

This is Governor Brady, over Pentonville.'

'Oh yeah?'

'I have a chappie on B wing, might be of interest to you.'

'Why?'

'You are still in charge of the Umpire investigation, aren't you?' A note of petulance crept in as he added: 'I mean you are interested in solving the cricket business?'

'Of course, absolutely. I'm sorry, it's been a long day.'

'Try a day in the Ville sometime.'

Roberts wanted to shout: 'Get on with it, fuckhead,' but he knew the butter approach was vital, and with a trowel, said: 'You do a terrific job there, Governor, it can't be easy.'

'That's for sure.'

'So, this man you've got, you think he might be our boy?'

'He says he is.'

'Oh.'

'Came in yesterday on a GBH. We had to stick him on B because of his psychotic behaviour.'

'Might I come see?'

'I'll be waiting.'

When Roberts put down the phone, he didn't feel any hope. They were up to their asses in Umpires, all nutters and all bogus. But he'd have to check it out.

As Brant parked the car, he said: 'This Volvo is like my ex.'

'Yes?'

'Too big and too heavy.'

'Gosh, I wonder why she left you.'

The maître d' made a fuss of them, placed them at the best table, said: 'Always glad to be of service to our police.'

Fiona sighed. The restaurant was near full and a hum of conversation carried. Two huge menus were brought. She said: 'You order.'

'Okey-dokey.'

A young waiter danced over and gave them a smile of dazzling fellowship. Brant asked: 'What's the joke, pal?'

'*Scusi?*'

'Jeez, another wop. Give us a minute, will yer?' A less

hearty withdrawal from the waiter. Fiona said: 'You have such magnetism.'

'That's me all right.' Then he clicked his fingers, said: 'Yo, Placedo!' And ordered thus: starters, prawn cocktails; main, marinated Tweed salmon with cucumber salad and a pepper steak, roast and jacket potatoes; dessert, pecan sponge pie with marmalade ice-cream; wine, three bottles of Chardonnay.

The waiter looked astonished and Brant said: 'Hey, wake up, Guiseppe, it won't come on its own.'

Fiona didn't know what to say, said: 'I dunno what to say.'

'Yer man, light on his feet I'd say.'

'Excuse me?'

'An arse bandit, one of them pillow biters.'

'Oh God.'

The food began to arrive, and the first bottle of wine. Brant poured freely, raised his glass, said: 'A toast.'

'Good heavens.'

'That too.'

She was glad of the alcohol and drank full, asked: 'Do you hate my husband so much?'

'What?'

'You must do. I mean, all this.'

'He's a good copper and straight. This isn't to do with him.'

'Why, then? Surely it's not just a fuck.'

He winced at her obscenity, put his glass down slowly, then said: 'It's about class. I never had none. You have it. I thought it might rub off.'

'You can't be serious.'

> 'You wouldn't kill me in cold
> blood, would you?'
> 'No, I'll let you warm up
> a little.'

Paul Guilfoyle and James Cagney, White Heat

He spooned the prawn cocktail as if it contained secrets, then looked her straight in the eye, began: 'I think I was born angry and there was plenty to be pissed about. We had nowt. Then I became a copper and guess what?' She hadn't a clue but he wasn't expecting an answer, continued: 'I mellowed 'cos I got respect at last. It felt like I was somebody. Me and Mike Johnson. He was me best mate, Mickey, bought the act even more than I did. Believed yer public could give a toss about us. One night he went to sort out a domestic, usual shit, old man beating the bejaysus out of his missus. Mickey got him up against the wall, we were putting the cuffs on him, when the wife laid him out with a rolling pin.' Brant laughed out loud, heads turned, he repeated: 'A bloody rolling pin, like a bad joke.'

'Was he hurt?'

'He was after they castrated him.'

Fiona dropped her spoon, said: 'Oh, good grief.'

'Good don't come into it. See, you gotta let 'em see you're the most brutal fuckin' thing they've ever seen. They come quiet then.' Brant was deep in memory, even his wine was neglected.

'My missus. I loved her but I couldn't let 'er know. Couldn't go soft, know what I mean? Else I'd end up singing soprano like old Mickey.'

Whatever Fiona might have said, could have said, was averted. Brant's bleeper went off, he said: 'Fuck,' and went to use the phone. A few moments later, he was back. 'There's heat going on in Brixton, I gotta go.'

'Oh.'

He rummaged in his pockets, dumped a pile of notes on the table, said: 'I've called a cab for you, you stay, finish the grub,' and then he was gone. Fiona wanted to weep. For whom or why, she wasn't sure, but a sadness of infinity had shrouded her heart.

As Brant approached the car, his mind was in a swirl of pain through memory. He'd let his guard down, and now he struggled to regain the level of aggression that was habitual. As a mantra, he mouthed Jack Nicholson's line from *A Few Good Men*: 'The truth, you can't handle the truth – I eat breakfast every day, four hundred yards from Cubans who want to kill me.' For a moment he was Jack Nicholson, shoving it loud into the face of Tom Cruise.

It worked. The area of vulnerability began to freeze over, and the smile, slick in its satanic knowledge, began to form. He said: 'I'm cookin' now, mister.' And he was. As the Volvo lurched towards south-east London, Nicholson's lines fired on: 'You come down here in your faggoty white uniforms, flash a badge and expect me to salute.'

Last train to Clarkesville

As Roberts was resigning himself to a haul to Pentonville, the phone rung again. He considered ignoring it, but finally said: 'Damn and blast,' and picked it up. 'Yes?'

'Is that the police?'

'Yes.' (very testy)

'This is the nursing sister at St Thomas'.'

'And?'

'Well, I don't know if I'm being fanciful, but we have a man here who… I don't know how to say this.'

Roberts exhaled loudly and said: 'You have the cricket murderer, am I right?' He could hear her amazement and it was a moment before she could say: 'Yes. Yes, at least it might be.'

Roberts couldn't contain his sarcasm, said: 'Confessed, did he?'

'Not exactly, no. A man was brought in after being hit by a bus, and in his sleep, he was shouting things that were peculiar.'

Roberts felt he had been hit by a bus himself, said wearily: 'I'll get someone over there toot sweet.'

'Toot what?'

'Soon, sister, OK?'

'All right, I'll expect you.'

'Yeah, yeah.'

And he rung off. He rooted in his pocket, took out a coin, said: 'Heads the 'Ville, tails the other monkey.'

Flipped it high.

It was heads.

Officers had blocked off Electric Avenue. Brant could see armed officers lining up along the roofs. Falls came running, said: 'You got my call?'

'I owe you, babe. Is this what I think it is?'

'Someone reported a barrage of shots and a local PC went to investigate. He narrowly escaped having his head shot off.' Brant approached the officer in charge, said: 'I think I know who's inside. What's the status?'

'A bloody shambles. We know it's a dope pad, and four white men were seen going in. Then the shooting started. Nobody's come out. We have a negotiator on the way and we are trying to set up a phone link.'

Brant turned and said to Falls: 'Watch this.'

Before anyone could react, he walked across the street and into the building. The scene-of-crime guy exclaimed: 'What the hell?'

Brant made no effort to sneak up the stairs, but walked loudly, turned into a dimly lit corridor. The smell of cordite was thick, and something else, the smell of blood.

Kev was slouched against a wall, his legs spread out. He held a gun in each hand, not aimed but lying loosely on his chest. He was covered in blood.

Brant said: 'Shop!'

A lazy smile from Kev, then: 'You should've seen it, mate. We got in and told the fucks not to move. You know what they did?'

'They moved?'

'Started bleedin' shouting. At me brother, he got it in the neck. And Doug, well, he got it everywhere. I dunno about Fenton, I kinda lost him in the excitement.'

'Are you hurt bad?'

'I dunno, I don't feel nuffin'… bit tired I suppose.'

'You are the 'E' mob, right?'

'Yeah, that's us.'

'Tell you son, you done good, had us going a bit.'

'We did, didn't we?'

Brant edged closer, said: 'Thing is, whatcha gonna do now?'

'I dunno, mate.'

A little nearer. 'If you give it up boyo, you'll be famous. Lots of press, movie rights, mini-series, books. Jeez, you'll be on T-shirts.'

Very close now.

Kev began to move the gun in his right hand, and Brant smashed his foot into Kev's face. Then bounced his head against the wall a few times, pulled the guns away, said: 'That's all she wrote.'

He straightened up and slowly approached the flat, took a peek inside, muttered: 'Jesus!'

Moved in and stepped carefully over bodies. Saw a heavy wedge of banded cash and said: 'I'll be 'aving that.'

He pushed open the window, let himself be clearly seen, and shouted: 'All clear!'

After the clean-up process had begun, Brant was sitting in a police van, sipping tea from a styrofoam beaker. Falls walked over, said: 'Hear the buzz?'

'What? No, is it sirens?'

'No, sarge, it's a White Arrest.'

Brant said: 'I've been accused of all sorts of stuff. Some of it stuck, some of it's even true and none I'll admit to. But, hand on my heart, I've never been a racist. So, I can honestly say, you're the first nigger I ever liked.'

Falls didn't know whether to assault him or plain ignore him. Instead: 'Well, Sergeant, perhaps you're not as black as you're painted.' It was the closest they'd come to camaraderie.

Roberts emerged from Pentonville spitting anger. The suspect was a complete wash out. So loaded on Thorazine he confessed to being Lord Lucan.

It took all of Roberts' patience not to wallop him. Worse,

he had had to brown-nose the Governor, who said: 'Can't be too careful, eh?'

'Exactly.'

As he got in his car, he thought he'd have time to swing by St Thomas', then said: 'Fuck that for a game of soldiers.'

Fiona answered the phone, wondered if it was Brant, said: 'Yes?'

'Fiona, this is Penny.'

'What do you want?'

'Oh Fiona, I'm so sorry, but I had no choice.'

'That's not quite right, you chose, but you chose to save yourself.'

'Can you ever forgive me?'

'I shouldn't think so.'

'What can I do to make up for it? Anything. I'll do anything.'

'Would you?'

'Oh yes.'

'Then go fuck yourself, you've done it to everybody else.'

Two weeks later

At St Thomas' Hospital, the doctor was releasing his patient. 'Now Mr Shannon, will you take it easy?'
'Is sport OK?'
'Purely as a spectator, is that clear?'
'Crystal,' and the Umpire smiled.

The furore of the Brixton shoot-out was ebbing. Commendations, awards, lavish praise, expected promotion: all followed Brant's way. The George Medal was being mentioned.

Brant was coming home after yet another evening of liquid congratulation. Outside his building, he let back his head and muttered: 'Ain't life grand?'

A woman approached and asked: 'Change for tea, mistah?'

Too late he registered the band-aid, and a knife went deep into his lower back.

As he fell to his knees, he thought: 'Ahh... bollocks.'

Roberts checked again in the full-length mirror. He was dressed in a tight black shirt, homburg on his head, and dark shades. Oh yeah, and white socks, meeting the too-short pants. Brant had finally talked him into the idea for the fancy dress at the Met dance. When Fiona saw him, she gasped: 'What on earth?'

'I'm a Blues Brother!'

'You look like a spiv.'

And she'd retreated in gales of laughter. When Brant had

explained, it seemed more feasable. How they'd burst into the hall, light shining behind them. Before anyone could recover, they'd launched into an improvised version of a) 'Rawhide' or:b) 'Stand By Your Man' ('As long as it's loud, Guv').

Roberts readjusted the shades and said tentatively: 'We're...'

No!

'We're on...'

Better. And finally, out loud and proud:

'We're on a mission from God.'

The Do-Not Press
Fiercely Independent Publishing

www.thedonotpress.com

All our books are available in good bookshops or –
in the event of difficulty – direct from us at the cover
price (UK and Europe only):
The Do-Not Press Limited, Dept AWA,
16 The Woodlands
London
SE13 6TY
(UK)

If you do not have Internet access you can write to
us at the above address in order to join our mailing
list and receive fairly regular news on new books
and offers. Please mark your card 'No Internet' or
'Luddite'.